The I

Steve Carper
Peter Enfantino
Emily Hockaday
Gary Lovisi
Rick McCollum
Marc Myers
Vince Nowell, Sr.
Jack Seabrook
Robert Snashall
Bob Vojtko
Joe Wehrle, Jr.

Edited by Richard Krauss

The Digest Enthusiast (TDE) Book Thirteen
Published twice a year by Larque Press LLC

Editor/Designer: Richard Krauss
Cover: Brian Buniak
Cartoons: Bob Vojtko (pages 60, 77, and 142)

Printed on demand from December 2020 in the United States of America
and other countries.

Larque Press LLC
4130 SE 162nd Court
Vancouver, WA 98683

Visit <larquepress.com> for news about current digest magazines and vintage digest
covers. Join our mailing list for exclusive updates on *The Digest Enthusiast* and other
Larque Press projects. Sign up at <larquepress.com>

Back Cover Images
Space on Earth by Emily Hockaday 2019
Murder Mystery Monthly No. 18 1944
The Original Science Fiction Stories July 1958
Manhunt Detective Story Monthly March 1955
Mystery Book Magazine No. 19 May 1947
Falcon Books No. 36 1952

Our thanks to our contributors for some of the cover images that appear in this edition.
Cover images are retouched to remove defects from the original source material. When
reference material is not available, retouched areas are "best guess." In some cases text may
be reset in a font similar to the original work.

Opposite: Nov/Dec 2020 issues of *Analog* and *Asimov's*
Managing Editor: Emily Hockaday

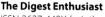
The Digest Enthusiast
ISSN 2637-448X (print)
ISSN 2637-4498 (Kindle)
ISBN 978-1-716-34158-8

 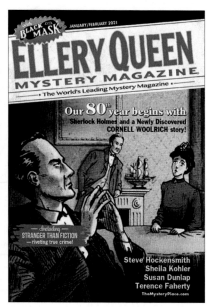

Jan/Feb 2021 issues of *Asimov's Science Fiction* and *Ellery Queen Mystery Magazine.*

News Digest

Emily Hockaday: Asimov's

For 2021, *Asimov's* has an exciting year planned, including novellas from **Greg Egan, Robert Reed, Alex Irvine**, and **David Moles.** Short stories and novelettes include pieces by **Felicity Shoulders, Ray Nayler, Kali Wallace, James Patrick Kelly, Derek Künsken**, and more! *Asimov's* is also happy to introduce **Sheree Renée Thomas** as our newest book reviewer! Her first review will appear in the May/June issue.

Rick Ollerman:
Down & Out: The Magazine

The sixth edition of *Down & Out: The Magazine* is complete and in the hands of its publisher, Down & Out Books, and could be out at any time.

Jackie Sherbow: Ellery Queen

In 2021, *EQMM* will be celebrating its eightieth year! The January/February issue celebrates Sherlock Holmes's birthday with Holmesian tales by **Terence Faherty, Josh Pachter, Mike Adamson**, and **Steve Hockensmith**. The issue also contains a story in translation featuring **Marcel Aymé's** detective known as "the French Sherlock Holmes" and a newly discovered, previously unpublished story by **Cornell Woolrich.** Our March/April issue features stories by 2020 Readers Award winner **David Dean** and best-selling author **Charlaine Harris,** and the first appearance of **Mickey Spillane's** iconic character Mike Hammer in *EQMM* (in a previously unpublished tale adapted by

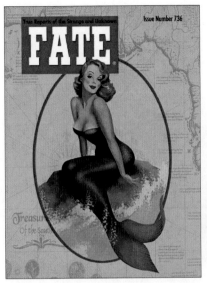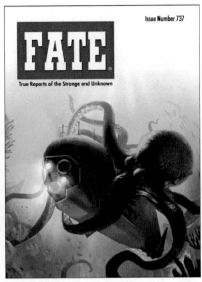

Preliminary covers for the upcoming *Fate* magazines No. 736 and No. 737.

Updates from the Editors, Writers, and Artists of today's newsstand and indie digest magazines.

Max Allan Collins from a Spillane movie script). May/June will feature an eightieth-anniversary tribute to longtime fans, a novella by multiple *EQMM* Readers Award winner and Edgar winner **Doug Allyn**, and stories by seveal other award winners, including **Lauren James**.

Phyllis Galde: Fate Magazine

We are working hard on the next issue with amazing articles on Mermaids, Tesla, When Walls Bleed, Hands of Death, and much more.

Gary Lovisi: Paperback Parade

The current issue of *Paperback Parade*, No. 109, is available now. It has articles on UK cover artist **Peff**, author **Roy Huggins**, Winthrop Press cigarette paperbacks,

I, The Jury, **Alfred Bester** SF paperbacks, UK Tit-Bits SF, and more.

Gary's new Sherlock Holmes story "The Moriarity Obsfuscation" is in the new book Sherlock Holmes Consulting Detective No. 15, out now from Airship27.

Gary has also written the introduction for the great new Stark House Press edition of two hard crime noir reprints of Lion Books by **G.H. Otis**, *Bourbon Street* and *Hot Cargo*.

Scotch Rutherford: Switchblade Magazine

November saw release of *Switchblade* 13. It's definitely more of a gutter noir issue than 12 is. In the Editor's corner for the print edition of *SB* 13, I talk about

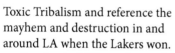

Paperback Parade No. 109 Nov. 2020.

Sherlock Holmes Consulting Detective No. 15.

Toxic Tribalism and reference the mayhem and destruction in and around LA when the Lakers won.

Starting in 2020, we dropped down to two issues a year. Issue 13 marks the end of *Switchblade* Volume One. In 2021, we will not be doing any numbered issues, only Special Issues. The first of which will be *Switchblade: Los Angeles*. Submissions for *SB: LA* will open up in April 2021. You do not need to be an LA resident. You simply need to write a good *Switchblade*-style crime story set in the city of angels. Special consideration will be given to LA stories that can be shot (filmed) on a modest budget—more details on that, in April. *SB:LA* will have a June/July release. The theme of the second Special Issue for 2021 will be revealed in June 2021. Also on the horizon (although, sadly there is no timeframe on its arrival) is *Switchblade: Choice*

Cuts, what you might call a *Switchblade* greatest hits, Volume One.

In regards to the pandemic restricting the activities of *Switchblade* magazine: I can't (or won't because I'm a paranoid germaphobe) do photoshoots with models for cover art or apparel ads. A minor thing. As far as the live readings, I had already handed those over to **Rick Risemberg**. (you might've seen his name—he's in a few *SB* issues) The first event Rick scheduled almost happened right when the Covid lockdown hit. So if things ever get back to normal, it'll be Rick who will be hosting the SB live events.

All Due Respect 2020

All twelve issues of 2020's online magazine are collected in the print volume: *All Due Respect 2020*, edited by **Chris Rhatigan** and **David Nemeth**. It's an outstanding collection of top indie crime fiction

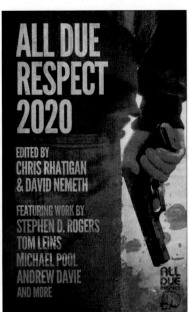

Switchblade Magazine No. 13 Nov. 2020.

All Due Respect 2020.

writers from All Due Respect Books, an imprint of Down & Out Books.

Michael Bracken: Black Cat Mystery Magazine, Guns + Tacos, etc.

We've been working hard to get *BCMM* back on a quarterly schedule, and in September we released issue 7, our special P.I. issue.

Black Cat Mystery Magazine No. 8 (due out in December), includes stories by: **D.V. Bennett**, **John M. Floyd**, **Barb Goffman**, **John Hegenberger**, **M.A. Monnin**, **Elizabeth Zelvin**, and a classic reprint.

BCMM 9 (due out in March), includes stories by: **Ann Aptaker**, **Michael Bracken**, **Elliot Capon**, **John M. Floyd**, **James A. Hearn**, **Michael Kurland**, **B.A. Paul**, **Cynthia Ward**, **Stacy Woodson**, and a classic reprint.

BCMM 10 (due out in June), includes stories by: **Emilio DeGrazia**, **Barb Goffman**, **Tom Larsen**, **Janice Law**, **Steve Liskow**, **R.S. Morgan**, **Gregory L. Norris**, **Mark Troy**, **Elizabeth Zelvin**, and a classic reprint.

In March, *BCMM* opens for submissions for a special all-cozy issue, which will likely be *BCMM* 12, due out in December 2021. Sometime after we close the reading period for the cozy issue, we will open up to general submissions.

Guns + Tacos

Season 2 of *Guns + Tacos* wraps up in December of this year. The six novellas, released as individual ebooks, will be collected and released as a pair of paperbacks in early 2021. Contributors include: **Ann Aptaker**, **Eric Beetner**, **Alec Cizak**, **Ryan Sayles**, **Mark Troy**, **Michael Bracken/Trey R. Barker**, and a bonus story for subscribers only by **Trey R. Barker**.

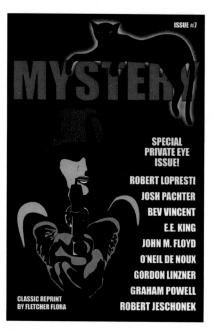

Black Cat Mystery Magazine No. 7 Sept. 2020.

Guns + Tacos Season. 2 Episode 9 Aug. 2020.

We have novellas in hand for Season 3, which releases in the last half of 2021, and we'll announce those contributors later.

Jukes & Tonks

Co-edited with **Gary Phillips**, *Jukes & Tonks* releases April 19 from Down & Out Books. Contributors include: **Trey R. Barker, Michael Bracken, Jonathan Brown, S.A. Cosby, John M. Floyd, Debra H. Goldstein, Gar Anthony Haywood, Penny Micklebury, Gary Phillips, William Dylan Powell, Kimberly Richardson**, and **Stacy Woodson**.

Mickey Finn: 21st Century Noir.

Vol. 1 releases December 2020, Vol. 2 in December 2021, and I start reading submissions for Vol. 3 in January.

On a personal note, I have stories due out the first half of 2021 in: *Only the Good Die Young*

(stories inspired by the songs of **Billy Joel**), *The Great Filling Station Holdup* (stories inspired by the songs of **Jimmy Buffett**), and *Bullets and Other Hurting Things* (a **Bill Crider** tribute anthology).

And stories forthcoming (but no confirmed pub dates yet) in: *AHMM, EQMM, Close to the Bone, Unnerving,* and *Mystery Tribune.*

Jennifer Landels: Pulp LIterature

Pulp Literature Issue 28, Autumn 2020:

Under the watchful gaze of **Ashley-Rose Goentaro's** Faery Godmother, memories are writ large in short fiction from **Renée Sarojini Saklikar, Dawn Lo, Weiwei Xu**, and **Soramimi Hanarejima**, and stars and moons illuminate stories by **James Dorr** and **David Milne**. Poetry comes from the Magpie Award winners **Charlene Kwiatkowski, Maria Ford**, and **Cara Waterfall**, a

Pulp Literature No. 28 Autumn 2020.

Nostalgia Digest Winter 2021.

puzzle from SiWC contest winner **Cameron MacDonald**, and humour from **Susan Pieters**, while heroines Toinette and Frankie Ray return us to 17th century France and 1930s Hollywood with **JM Landels** and **Mel Anastasiou**.

Coming up in Winter 2021: **Kris Sayer's** mischievous cover goat leads us into lands of myth and mystery with short fiction from **Shashi Bhat**, **SL Leong**, **Brandon Crilly**, **Erin Wagner**, and **KT Wagner**. The winners of the Hummingbird contest alight, Allaigna returns with **JM Landels**, and Frankie Ray's troubles deepen under **Mel Anastasiou's** pen.

Later in 2021 watch for fiction from **Robert Silverberg**, **Leo X Robertson**, **Claire Lawrence**, **Brenda Carre**, and **Zandra Renwick** with art from **Weiwei Xu**, **Tatjana Mirkov-Popovicki**, and **Matthew Nielsen**.

Steve Darnall: Nostalgia Digest

The Winter 2021 issue of *Nostalgia Digest* features a cover story about the remarkable life and career of **Olivia de Havilland**, Hollywood legend and legal pioneer, along with articles about the screen partnership of **Nelson Eddy** and **Jeanette MacDonald**, the many voices of *The Shadow,* comedian and philanthropist **Danny Thomas**, radio's first star newsman, memories of mimeograph machines and more—including the schedule for the weekly radio show *Those Were the Days.*

Emily Hockaday: Analog

In 2021, *Analog* continues its tenth decade with a new, sleek logo [see page 34], and a stuffed inventory including authors like **Adam-Troy Castro**, **Marie Vibbert**, **Frank Wu**, **Brenda Kalt**, **Tom Jolly**, **Catherine Wells**, **Neal Asher**, **Rosemary Claire Smith**, and many

Fantasy & Science Fiction Nov/Dec 2020.

Fantasy & Science Fiction Jan/Feb 2021, the final issue edited by C.C. Finlay.

more. *Analog* also has a series of special features on the roster, as well as the usual fascinating fact articles.

Gordon Van Gelder: F&SF

Sheree Renée Thomas has been named the new editor of *The Magazine of Fantasy & Science Fiction*, taking over with the March/April 2021 issue. She replaces **C.C. Finlay**, who will be stepping down to devote more time to writing.

C.C. Finlay's writing career began with frequent appearances in *Fantasy & Science Fiction*, publishing more than twenty stories in the magazine between 2001 and 2014, earning Hugo, Nebula, Sturgeon, and Sidewise Award nominations, along with four novels, a collection, and stories in numerous other magazines and anthologies. In January 2015, he was announced as the new editor of the magazine

and took over officially with the March/April issue. His tenure as editor is the fourth longest in the magazine's history, following **Ed Ferman**, **Gordon Van Gelder**, and **Anthony Boucher**. The January/February 2021 issue will be his last.

Sheree Renée Thomas is the award-winning writer and editor of *Dark Matter: A Century of Speculative Fiction from the African Diaspora* (2000) and *Dark Matter: Reading the Bones* (2004), which earned the 2001 and 2005 World Fantasy Awards for Year's Best Anthology. She has also edited for Random House and for magazines like *Apex*, *Obsidian*, and *Strange Horizons*. Widely anthologized, her work also appears in *The Big Book of Modern Fantasy* and *The New York Times*. She was honored as a 2020 World Fantasy Award Finalist for her contributions to the genre.

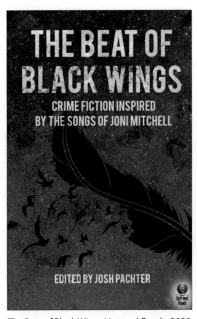

The Beat of Black Wings Untreed Reads, 2020.

The Further Misadventures of Ellery Queen
Wildside Press, 2020.

Thomas will be the tenth editor in *The Magazine of Fantasy & Science Fiction's* storied history. Her first appearance on the masthead will be in the March/April 2021 issue.

Josh Pachter

The appearance of my "The Adventure of the Red Circles" in the Jan/Feb 2020 issue made me the first and only person to appear in *EQMM* in seven consecutive decades. In May, I received the Short Mystery Fiction Society's Edward D. Hoch Memorial Golden Derringer Award for Lifetime Achievement and became the first and only person to receive a Golden Derringer and win a competitive Derringer in the same year (with my "The Two-Body Problem" from *Mystery Weekly* taking the Best Flash category).

Also in 2020, I had another story ("The Adventure of the Black-and-Blue Carbuncle," Nov/Dec) in *EQMM*, two in *Mystery Weekly* ("The Pig is Committed" in April and "The Odds Are Good" in August), and one each in *Mystery Tribune* ("Paramus is Burning," No. 13), *Black Cat Mystery Magazine* ("The Stopwatch of Death," No. 7), *Down and Out: The Magazine* ("The Stonewall Jackson Death Site," Vol. 2 No 2), the Chessie Chapter of Sisters in Crime's *Invitation to Murder* ("Muggins," Wildside Press), *Mickey Finn: 21st-Century Noir* ("Better Not Look Down," Down and Out Books), and *The Beat of Black Wings: Crime Fiction Inspired by the Songs of Joni Mitchell* ("The Beat of Black Wings," Untreed Reads).

I edited *The Beat of Black Wings* (Untreed) and *The Misadventures of Nero Wolfe* (Mysterious Press) and co-edited *The Further Misadventures of Ellery Queen* (Wildside

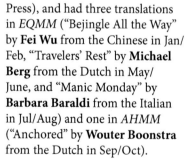

The Dark City Oct. 2020.

Mystery Weekly Magazine Dec. 2020.

Press), and had three translations in *EQMM* ("Bejingle All the Way" by **Fei Wu** from the Chinese in Jan/Feb, "Travelers' Rest" by **Michael Berg** from the Dutch in May/June, and "Manic Monday" by **Barbara Baraldi** from the Italian in Jul/Aug) and one in *AHMM* ("Anchored" by **Wouter Boonstra** from the Dutch in Sep/Oct).

Coming up, I have a story in *EQMM* in Jan/Feb 2021 ("The Five Orange Pipes") and a story ("The City of Light") and a translation ("A Bucharest Arrest" by **Bogdan Hrib** from the Romanian) in Mar/Apr, plus a story in *Mystery Weekly* ("The Night Movers"). And there are two new anthologies I've edited coming out in the spring: *The Great Filling Station Holdup: Crime Fiction Inspired by the Songs of Jimmy Buffett* (Down and Out Books) and *Only the Good Die Young: Crime Fiction Inspired by the*

Songs of Billy Joel (Untreed Reads). Plus more later in the year . . .

John Betancourt: Sherlock Holmes Mystery Magazine

Editor **Marvin Kaye** is not reading submissions at the moment (and probably not for all of 2021, since he is overstocked.) We anticipate a return to normal schedule in 2021, with 4 issues scheduled.

The Dark City

The October 2020 edition of *The Dark City Magazine* includes crime and mystery stories by **Natalie Harris-Spencer**, **D.C. Koch**, **Peter Emmett Naughton**, **Michael Zimecki**, and **Scott Edelman**. The series is edited by **Steve Oliver**.

Chuck Carter: Mystery Weekly Magazine

The pandemic has not affected our sales much one way or another. I've read posts online from other publishers and authors who claim their sales have increased after Covid-19 appeared, but I haven't noticed any increase or drop-off.

Here is the line-up of authors for *Mystery Weekly Magazine* Jan. 2021: **Brendan DuBois, R.T. Lawton, Josh Pachter, Anne Swardson, Alan Orloff, Caleb Coy, Mike McHone,** and **Vy Kava.**

Justin Marriott: The Paperback Fanatic

The 9th edition of *The Sleazy Reader* was released during the final production of this issue of *TDE*. It include coverage of 50s crime digests and **Harlan Ellison's** digest work in the crime genre—a must-have issue for digest enthusiasts. **Contents includes:**

- Gangster biographies from Monarch Books and their Americana line
- Belmont Tower laugh in the face of copyright laws with this cheekily named line of Mafia biographies
- A visual guide to sleazy crime digests
- Wise Guy **Sean Nodland** on **Peter McCurtin**, editor and writer at Belmont Tower
- Plundering EC Comics and cocking a snook to good taste, it's Fight Against Crime!
- Pontiac Publishing and their wild line of crime digests
- **John Marr** of *Murder Can Be Fun* on the most famous of all true-crime magazines
- 'Mr Crime' **Sean Nodland** on *Crime Does Not Pay* comics
- **Harlan Ellison's** stories for the sleazy crime digests
- The early 70s series that added hardcore sex and violence to the crime novel

The Seazy Reader No. 9 Nov. 2020.

- **Scott Carlson** obsessively scans decades old Kiwi legal documents—so that you don't have to
- **Roy Nugen** on the original Travis (clue: it isn't McGee)

Next up is 'Blazing Conflict: From WW1 to 'Nam, war as depicted in paperbacks and comics'. Will contain 150+ reviews of paperbacks and comics which dealt with war as their central theme. As well as essays on key titles and authors. Scheduled for early Summer 2021.

Doug Draa: Weirdbook

No concrete news to report except this successful title will continue for at least eight more issues and the next themed annual will center on zombies.

Bob Vojtko: Cartoonist

Besides his cartoons appearing in every issue of *TDE* and *Pulp Modern*, Bob Vojtko's cartoons are featured in *Reader's Digest*,

New Bob Vojtko mini comics: *Low Budet Funnies* No. 11, *Fake Comics* No. 1, and *Butrum Beaver* No. 1.

The Saturday Evening Post, Funny Times, Women's World, and many other newsstand magazines. When he's not creating new gag cartoons, chances are he's drawing mini comics. Some of his recent minis include *Butrum Beaver, Bent Lemons, Headless Hal, Fake Comics*, and his latest *Low Budget Funnies* No. 11. Only $1 each. Contact him via his Facebook page to get your copies. <facebook.com/bob.vojtko.7>

Michael Neno: Comic Creator

Two new public domain tiny mashup microcomics available for purchase from Michael Neno:
1) *Tune Time Presents: The Stuck-Inside Song*. The first quarantine microcomic in existence, is a mashup, madcap comedy musical! 20 pages, full color, signed upon request.
2) *After Hours He-Man Antics*. Watch as brave men tangle with killer cats! Witness the high-flying alli-

Elephant No. 4 and *A Traveller's Guide to Eight Wonders of the Ancient World* by Marc Myers.

Mulmig No. 3 by Marc Myers.   Two recent public doman microcomics by Michael Neno.

gator drop! See depraved guard dogs maul expensive beef jerky! 24 pages, full color, signed upon request. These microcomics are $4 each (ppd.). Order these and other mini-comics and zines via PayPal from: <www.nenoworld.com/Minicomics. html> or mail check or cash to:

    M.R. Neno Productions
    P.O. Box 307675
    Gahanna, OH 43230

Marc Myers: Artist/Publisher

See Marc's latest collage illustrating **Bob Snashall's** story "Gaslight Unrolling of the Stars" on page 130.

In 2017, Marc published a 156-page collection of comix by **Clark Dissmeyer**, called *Through a Basement Window*. This year, he's completed editing his first hardcover book, *Oddities and Other Grotesques*, that collects over 150 pages of comix and zines by the late **Roman Scott**. The volume includes recollections by Marc, **Jonathan Falk**, **Todd Mecklem**, and **Marcus Reed**. The volume is available now for $20 at <lulu.com>

Marcs most recent collage zines are *Traveller's Guide to the Eight Wonders of the Ancient World*, *Elephant* 4, and *Mulmig* 3. For

sale or trade send email to: muckmires@hotmaill.com

Peter Enfantino: Cimarron Press

In its first full year of business, Cimarron Street Books published four issues of *bare•bones* magazine (the latest being a monster-sized special issue featuring a dissection of media monsters Konga, Reptilicus and Gorgo; a look at **Val Lewton's** horror films; and **Richard Krauss's**

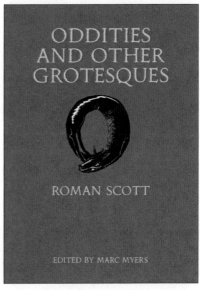

Roman Scott's *Oddities and Other Grotesques*, edited by Marc Myers 2020.

bare•bones No. 4 Fall 2020.

is called *Cool It Down*, and will be released in early 2021.

Pulp Modern will be celebrating its tenth anniversary in 2021 with two special, themed issues.

Pulp Modern is one of several publications joining up to create the Independent Fiction Alliance, a coalition designed to promote the work of independent writers and publishers and to safe guard free expression in the literary arts. The IFA is currently planning an anthology, the theme of which is currently under wraps. Folks should look for more info on the IFA in the early part of 2021.

Amazing Stories

The current incantation of *Amazing Stories* is a full-size magazine from Experimenter Publishing. The latest issue is Vol. 77 No. 2.

Jackie Sherbow: Alfred Hitchcock

AHMM's January/February 2021 celebrates the holidays and new year with stories by Edgar nominee **Stephen Ross** and multi award winner **Barb Goffman**, as well as a timely Mystery Classic by **Edgar Allan Poe**. March/April features tales by **Brendan DuBois**, **William Burton McCormick**, and **Melissa Yi**, as well as a Dr. Watson tale by **James Tipton**. In May/June, readers will find work by previous Black Orchid Novella Award winners **James Lincoln Warren**, **Robert Lopresti**, **Mark Thielman**, and **Mark Bruce**, as well as a new story by **John Lutz**.

Mike Chomko: PulpFest

Love will be in the air at PulpFest 2021. Shadows too!

PulpFest 2021 will celebrate the centennial of the best-selling pulp

dissection of *Verdict* magazine), a trade paperback collecting the best from the original incarnation of *bare•bones*, an oversize trade paperback of *The Best of The Scream Factory*, and five volumes of **David J. Schow's** writing (his non-fiction collection *Wild Hairs*, four short story collections including the first publication of *Monster Movies*, and the ground-breaking anthology Schow edited in the 80s: *Silver Scream*). For an encore, 2021 should see (at least) four more issues of *bare•bones*, another dozen Schow titles, a sister magazine titled *Dungeons of Doom* focusing on horror comics, and a few other surprises.

Alec Cizak: Uncle B Publications

The third book in my "Unholy Trio Trilogy" that started with *Down on the Street* and continued with *Breaking Glass*,

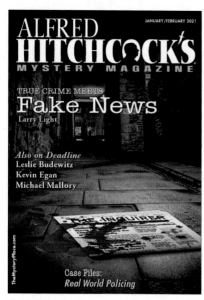

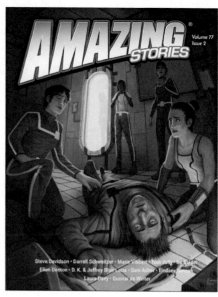

Alfred Hitchcock's Mystery Mag. Jan/Feb 2021.

Amazing Stories Vol. 77 No. 2 Sept. 2020.

magazine of all, Street & Smith's *Love Story Magazine.* The magazine debuted as a quarterly in the spring of 1921 and ran for nearly 1200 issues. In 1929, it was selling 600,000 copies each and every week.

Next year is also the ninetieth anniversary of another bestselling Street & Smith pulp. *The Shadow, A Detective Magazine* debuted in early 1931. It was the first hero pulp and spawned many imitators. *Doc Savage Magazine, The Phantom Detective, The Spider*, and *Secret Agent "X"* are just of few.

The convention will feature presentations on *Love Story* and the genre it inspired, and commemorate some of the top women pulp editors. It will also explore the artists who illustrated *The Shadow*, people who inspired or were inspired by the character, and the creators who chronicled The Shadow's storied career.

All this, plus a dealers' room

filled with thousands of pulps, digests, paperbacks, comic books, original art, men's adventure magazines, and other great collectibles.

PulpFest 2021 will take place from August 18–21 at the Double-Tree by Hilton Hotel Pittsburgh—Cranberry in Mars, Pennsylvania. To learn more about this great convention, please visit <www.pulpfest.com>. You'll also find PulpFest on Facebook, Twitter, and Instagram.

Greg Shepard: Stark House Press

As you know, *The Best of Manhunt* 2 came out this summer. If there is a No. 3, it won't be next year. **Jeff Verzimmer** is working on *The Manhunt Companion* with **Peter Enfantino** for a March 2021 release—and that's the last word I have on *Manhunt*. [See page 156 for covers.]

Jeff did create a new volume that is due any day from the printer:

A Beatnik Trio: *Like Crazy, Man* by **Richard E. Geis**, *The Far-Out*

The Best of Manhunt 2 (2020) and *A Beatnik Trio* (2021) edited by Jeff Vorzimmer, Stark House.

Ones by **Dell Holland**, and *Beat Girl* by **Bonnie Golightly**. Three wild and crazy novels from the Sexual Revolution of the 1960s. "These books don't have any literary pretension of defining what the beat movement was, but rather they reflect the places and period in which beatniks were prevalent."
–Jeff Vorzimmer, from his intro.

J.D. Graves: EconoClash Review

Currently reading through submissions from June and prepping issue 7 together for an early 2021 release. It features **Matthew X Gomez, J. Travis Grundon, A.M. Walley, Russell W. Johnson, Kevin Folliard, Scott Forbes Crawford, Simon Broder**, and **Mack Moyer**. It continues our tradition of quality cheap thrills with healthy doses of crime, thrillers, fantasies, and one western all brought to you by Down & Out Books. Celebrate the end of

2020 with the best release of 2021.

My thanks to the folks at the Independent Fiction Alliance (IFA) for their support and encouragement. Thanks also to our readers and contributors. This wouldn't happen without you. Please consider purchasing a book or two from our advertisers and the independent booksellers who stock *The Digest Enthusiast* like Bud's Art Books, Michael Chomko Books, and Modern Age Books. I'm grateful to readers who have rated and reviewed our past issues on amazon and Goodreads, and those who have shared or liked Larque Press blog posts from <larquepress.com> on social media: Facebook, Twitter, and Pinterest. God willing, we'll be back in six months.
–RK

Switchblade No. 12

Review by Richard Krauss

"Crime is at an all-time high in the city of Los Angeles. And the air is toxic. But I'm not talking about smog. It's a good time to be a criminal."

–Scotch Rutherford *Switchblade* No. 12 July 2020

Switchblade No. 12 opens with a cautionary verse from Russell Highland and a caustic editorial by Scotch Rutherford. Bleak times we're all trying to ride out, fractured by bits of good news that sneak through the uncertainty of daily diligence or disregard. Nonetheless, the twelfth *Switchblade* collection of misfits provides ample escape from this pandemic prison, with a noirish mix of reality and reverie.

Sharp & Deadly Short Fiction
Sorry Not Sorry
by E.F. Sweetman

How will a chick like Mary weather the pandemic? She sure as hell won't try to solve the world's problems, but she will take things like she always does—protecting herself behind a mask. Given time, she'll steal something from anyone willing to get close. "I have never been caught, I just deny, deny, deny." Then moves on. "Sorry Not Sorry" scrapes off two of her transitory relationships with Ivan the smoker and Pauline the drinker. He's first, with Pauline close behind—victims of fate or Mary—or both?

From Dusk to Blonde
by C.W. Blackwell

Sandra doesn't think much of her daughter. To start with, who names their daughter Larceny? The girl's younger brother, Brandon, got a better name, but it didn't help his longevity. While Mom mourns his murder in between highs from the couch in her trailer, Larceny yearns for revenge. Blackwell's terse prose ignites her vengeance like a burn barrel devouring trash.

Radio Sutch by Jon Zelazny

Aspiring film producer, Stamp, ingratiates himself into the biz on the coattails of his Oscar-worthy brother, Terry. The wannabe producer has his pipe dreams set on a rockumentary, so when pal Mike Shaw nudges him toward the "fantastic mad bastard of a rocker," Screaming Lord Sutch, an inciting incident blossoms. Stamp sleuths out Clifton Enterprises and hooks up with receptionist Anya Butler. When his swagger flops, Stamp chills and finally clicks. Before long, the pair is headed for the secret lair of Lord Sutch

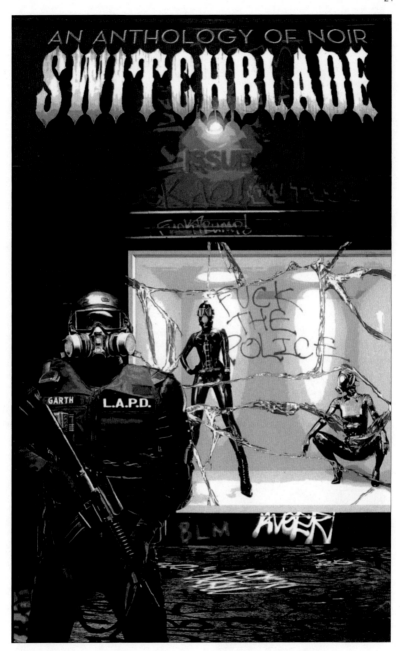

and his latest brain-strain, Radio Sutch, ripe for a theatrical release.

Forwarded Mail by D.K. Latta

A battered woman is horrified when she receives a package containing a severed finger. Could it be a piece of Jerry, her partner and abuser? No, the ring wrapped around this finger isn't his. Before she can stagger through her stupor, the phone rings. The unknown caller demands five hundred thousand in exchange for her husband. Tell no one. Further instructions will be given soon. The call ends. Still reeling, the woman realizes she isn't married.

Sealing the Deal
by Walter Sanville

According to Sir Andrew Likierman (*Harvard Business Review* Jan/Feb 2020) the elements of good judgment combine learning, trust, experience, detachment, options, and delivery. Of course, that's the clinical approach, devoid of circumstance. In a pinch, not all elements are equal. A dubious option may sound better than it ought to if the alternative is even worse. Lenny and Roach commiserate over their last coffees at a cafe some place in Tijuana—broke, friendless, and prospect-free. Some dude, two tables downwind, overhears their woes and presents an offer. "I know someone who needs a couple men to help crew a boat that's heading north. You interested?" They know it's a bad idea, but option-wise it's all they've got; and so in lies a criminally good story of drugs, murder, and high-seas misery.

A Dirty Hit by Elliott F. Sweeney

With a nod to the Gold Medal era, Sweeney baits ex-con Luke with a diner-dolly name of Roxy. "Short mousy hair, sharp cheeks, red lipgloss, a Gucci handbag; a black dress clinging to her like skin on a plum, and a pair of suede heels making her long legs even longer, like airport runways." His old cellmate warned Luke before his release to the bail hostel: no drugs, no skirts. Luke follows half of this sagely advice, but Roxy has other ideas; and poor Luke

is too busy thinking about her than why she would be interested in him.

Like a Diamond in the Sky
by William R. Soldan

Harold Detweiler has done well for himself. Really well. His patronage of a suburban health and wellness facility brings him into the purview of personal trainer Grady, an ex-con who's done everything he can to leave his petty theft and time served behind him. Trouble is, Deweiler flaunts his wealth and overshares his business. When Grady gives his pal Dante the low down, they decide to visit the rich man's abode while he's away for the week. An easy pinch soon turns into a bloody mess.

Aileen of Savanne Road
by Nathan Pettigrew

A hooker with a habit makes part-time attempts to raise her daughter, Aileen, between partying with boyfriends. After too many long years, the tart finally scores a promising mark in casino owner Mr. Val. Of course, the addled party pro fucks that up too, but by then Mr. Val has taken a shine to Miss Aileen and proceeds to show her the ropes on weapons, extortion, and payola. And Aileen learns fast.

They Call Me Cuban Pete
by Andrew Miller

Desi Arnaz hires a hit man to solve his extortion problem. Alternate reality or reasonable extrapolation? Doesn't matter. This engaging character piece is pure joy from start to finish. There's even a cameo with Lucille Ball.

Quick & Dirty Flash Fiction

The best short, short fiction delivers a sense of place (where and when), of tone (the voice and/or who), and a big reveal (how). My comments will focus on the first two and leave the climax for readers to enjoy on their own.

Henrietta's Calming Way

by Patrick Whitehurst

Henrietta's trip to Daniel's Corner Market aptly captures the stress and paranoia of shopping during a pandemic. Her attitude bristles with hostility and irritation as she plunges our vicarious ride-along toward its wrap-up

A Glitch in the Universe

by Albert Tucher

What a nice surprise to see Tucher's series character, Diana, in flash. He describes her on his website: "She needs to believe that she is the toughest, smartest woman in a hard, cold business. She's a prostitute who works behind closed doors, where the dangers can match those on the street. Two hundred dollars an hour may sound like a good payday, but sometimes it doesn't cover the damage." In this encounter, Diana finds herself in the clutches of a dirty cop who'd like nothing better than to see her dead.

The High Notes by Preston Lang

Who and what's in favor changes with who's in charge. What's celebrated by one megalomaniac is castigated by another. It's tempting to say it could only happen in organized crime, but that term has become far more inclusive in this era. Let's just say be very careful about what you say in front of today's boss.

Checking Out by Serena Jayne

A final look at crime in the pandemic places us in Melvyn's Multi-Mart. Masked shoppers curtail contamination and conceal identities when barren shelves tempt some to steal from others. If everyone is only for themselves are we left with retaliation or compassion—and what does it take to restore our humanity?

Person of Interest: Chris McGinley

Editor Scotch Rutherford conducts short interviews with essential indie authors in this feature that began in *Switchblade* No. 10. C.W. Blackwell and Alec Cizak are past participants. "Chris McGinley has been writing non stop for the past four years. He is a novelist, and short story author, with a strong penchant for Appalacian Noir." McGinley shares his thoughts on noir and influences in this three-page session. I believe McGinley's most recent story for *Switchblade* was "A Queen's Burial" in issue No. 8. This issue's authors and contributors are highlighted with bios and acknowledgements in the final five pages.

With twelve issues and two special editions, *Switchblade* has become a dependable haven for hard-hitting independent fiction. Its list of authors provides a who's who of rising stars of dark crime fiction. This edition adds further bloody evidence of its usual five-star killer status.

Switchblade No. 12
Editor: Scotch Rutherford
5" x 8" 186 pages
Print $7.99 Kindle $2.99
<switchblademag.com>

Emily Hockaday

Interviewed by Richard Krauss
Conducted via email in October 2020

"The phrase 'representation matters' is ubiquitous in our culture these days, because representation is such a powerful force for good."

–Emily Hockaday "Here There Be Women" *Analog* May/June 2020

The Digest Enthusiast: Describe your early introduction to fiction and your preferences.

Emily Hockaday: I have loved science fiction and fantasy as long as I can remember. In my recent editorial for *Analog's* 90th anniversary ("Here There Be Women," May/June 2020) I introduced the retrospective reprint "Weyr Search" by Anne McCaffrey and discussed the great impact her novels had on me as a young reader. She was my bridge from young adult to the adult section.

But at that point I was already well ensconced as an SFF fan. There are so many great SFF children's books out there! I loved Madeleine L'Engle, *Half Magic* by Edward Eager, *The Ear, the Eye, and the Arm* by Nancy Farmer, Susan Cooper's The Dark is Rising series, and almost everything Ray Bradbury had written. And of course, as a product of my era, I grew up on Goosebumps. I was a big reader and would devour whatever I could get my hands on.

TDE: Do you remember when you first discovered digests?

EH: My mother subscribed to *Reader's Digest*, and I started reading those pretty young. And while these aren't digests, I did start reading literary magazines as a child. I always had a subscription to whichever Cricket Media magazine was age appropriate, starting with *Ladybug* all the way up through *Cicada*. This instilled a lifelong love of fiction periodicals. (In fact, my three-year-old has subscriptions to both *Babybug* and *Ladybug* right now.)

TDE: At what point did your interest in reading expand to writing, and pursuit of a career in editing?

EH: I was always interested in writing. There are some seriously embarrassing fantasy stories and poems on some floppy disks and the hard drive of a long obsolete computer somewhere . . . .

I didn't gain experience editing other peoples' writing until college and grad school, where editorial commentary and insight was a huge component of student workshops. It is deeply satisfying to polish someone else's work and get it to its best possible place. My love of books and fiction, however, were the most necessary groundwork for becoming an editor.

After getting my MFA in poetry at NYU, I had two possible career tracks in mind that seemed equally

Hockaday's promotion to Associate Editor was first reflected in the May/June 2017 issues. *Analog* cover of Region NGC 6357 by NASA. *Asimov's* cover by Jim Simpson.

appealing: find a tenure-track instructor position or work in publishing. So I applied widely in both fields to entry-level positions. A friend alerted me to the opening at Dell (otherwise I may never have known of it!) and I was hired on as the editorial administrative assistant for the entire office. This job was a crash-course in publishing, as I filled various roles for all of the departments—including proofreading, drafting customer responses, writing columns and copy, answering phones, filing, and endless miscellaneous tasks. I worked for the numerous titles from the puzzles department, the four pulp titles (*Alfred Hitchcock*, *Ellery Queen*, *Analog* and *Asimov's*), and the *Dell Horoscope* magazine.

The science fiction department caught on pretty early that I was of a like mind, and when Stanley Schmidt retired and Trevor became editor of *Analog*, I was promoted to editorial assistant for the science fiction magazines only. Since then I've taken on the mantle of poetry editor for both magazines, launched social media, blogs, and podcasts for the magazines, coedited a mystery/SF horror anthology with managing editor Jackie Sherbow, and my title has changed to assistant editor, associate editor, and now managing editor.

TDE: As Managing Editor what are your what are your primary responsibilities?

EH: My first and foremost responsibility is to make sure the magazine gets assembled, isn't missing anything, and is sent to the printer. This includes monitoring deadlines, formatting and paginating the files, proofreading the final PDFs, and communicating with the art department, typesetting, and advertising. But ultimately that's a small fraction of the job. I copy and

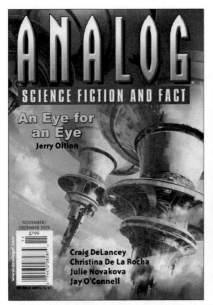
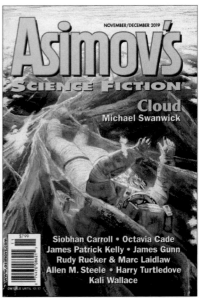

Hockaday's promotion to Managing Editor was first reflected in the Nov/Dec 2019 issues. *Analog* cover by Tuomas Korpi. *Asimov's* cover by Donato Giancola.

line edit each manuscript that appears in both *Asimov's* and *Analog*. I communicate with authors and columnists and proofreaders, and make sure everyone meets their targets and gets paid. As poetry editor, I read all poetry slush and choose which poems will appear in the magazine, handling any requested changes directly with the authors. Since 2016, when we launched social media for the magazines, I've been in charge of the blogs for each magazine while running the Twitter, Facebook, and Instagram accounts for both as well. This includes writing promotional copy, sharing vintage cover art, gathering guest posts for the blogs, and keeping generally tuned in to those inboxes. We also have podcasts that feature one free story from each issue. Our editorial assistant, Rae Purdom, has been invaluable in helping with the social media and our internet

presence. There are numerous other miscellaneous responsibilities that come up, but they are unpredictable. 2020 was *Analog's* 90th anniversary, for instance, and that required a more hands on approach to choosing cover art, which I helped editor Trevor Quachri with. To celebrate the anniversary, I coorganized the 4th annual City Tech Science Fiction Symposium with Professor Jason Ellis. That was a large but very satisfying undertaking, and one that will only come up once a decade! [See *TDE10* pgs 5 & 6]

TDE: Walk us through the development of an issue, from start to finish.

EH: First Sheila and Trevor read the slush, acquire stories, and work with the author on any large editorial changes. Then they land on my desk, where I copy and line edit them. Any queries I have for the authors I mark and set aside for

Analog May/June 2020 with Hockaday's Anniversary Retrospective Editorial and Anne McCaffrey's "Weyr Search."

later. After that I pass the stories along to our editorial assistant, Rae Purdom, who enters the corrections, formats the text, and does one last spell check on everything. Then Typesetting sets the Word documents into Quark (which is the program we make the final PDFs from), and now they are considered "first proofs." At this stage, Sheila or Trevor will decide on the contents of a particular issue and those files will zoom over to the proofreader. Simultaneously, any stories that will be illustrated either as the cover story or an interior spread are sent to the art department to be passed along to one of our artists.

(While the proofreader reviews this batch, and art gets started on illustrating, we begin working on the next issue!)

After the proofs come back from our proofreader, someone reviews their suggested corrections and either confirms them with a check or STETs them. For *Asimov's*, Sheila does this; for *Analog*, this is my responsibility.

Then the proofs—along with PDFs of the proofreader's pages—go to Typesetting for the second time. They make the corrections that we have okayed and then send us back the second proofs that have incorporated those changes.

At this point the authors get to see galleys of their stories. When we send these out, we revisit the queries that we had set aside earlier and get these addressed. Any typos or minor changes caught by the authors are made, and now the story is finally ready to have page numbers put in and folio lines updated with the correct issue date.

While all this has been going on, columns have been arriving, Brass Tacks has been compiled, and copy for the "Next Issue," "In Times To Come," and editorials are being written.

Now we have the makings of a complete issue. Around the time that galleys go out to authors, I create ad breakdown memos for our advertising department, so ad pages will be delivered around the time author changes come in. Art files arrive around that time, too.

We have one more exchange with typesetting—we send them the final Quark files to be made into PDFs. But before we send these files to type, we look over the "boards," carefully scrutinizing each page, making sure nothing is missing, and checking every department against the table of contents. Three sets of eyes will check these pages before we send them to Type. When Type turns these around this time, they are sending us the "Final" PDFs.

If we are still waiting on any last-minute ads or art (which does happen), this is when we must finalize those. We receive the "Final" PDFs and make PDFs ourselves of any missing pages.

This may seem redundant, but now we take one last look at the book in its entirety. Once again, three sets of eyes will look everything over. At this stage, I personally make a final memo that accounts for each page in the book, noting any filler or ads or art that may appear on those pages. I also have a checklist that I carefully go over to make sure I don't miss any easily overlooked errors. Despite all the levels of proofing, we do frequently find things that need to be changed.

After this last stage, I send the absolute final PDF files off to the printer and to the digital department for our electronic versions.

There is one last check that I perform on the printer's website once the files are uploaded there. This is more cursory and is merely to make sure no files were swapped or lost in the upload.

TDE: Is it fair to assume you work on more than one issue at a time? As of October 2020, which issues occupy your primary and secondary focus?

EH: Yes, we do work with long lead times. I always joke that I'm working in the future, so New Year never surprises me. At any given time, we are working on three issues—two actively, one passively. We are currently finalizing the very final PDFs for the January/February 2021 issues. These are due to the printer in early October. The

March/April issues are with their respective proofreaders, so those are the issues that are passive at the moment. And lastly, we are working on the May/June issues: Trevor and Sheila have been reading slush and compiling those issues and are just now getting them to me for copyediting. I already have a good stack of May/June stories for *Analog* that I'm getting started on.

TDE: Take us through the journey of a submission, perhaps one rejected along the way and another that is published. Are all stories submissions, or are some solicited?

EH: All of our submissions are sent through the magazines' respective submission portals. Essentially all of the stories chosen for publication are unsolicited. One exception: *Analog* solicited one story for the 90th anniversary year. But that is the first solicitation I have knowledge of in my almost ten years working for the magazines. The journey of a submission really depends on the submission, how caught up the editor is on slush, and whether or not the story needs rewrites and edits. A definite yes and a definite no will get a quicker turnaround from Sheila and Trevor. A story that is almost there but needs some work may linger a bit while the editors mull over where the story isn't working and how to articulate that to the writer. Then there will be some back and forth with the author before a contract is sent out.

TDE: How many submissions a month are typical?

EH: Monthly submissions fluctuate, but we usually receive somewhere around 750–800 each month.

TDE: What about poems?

EH: We get around 100 poetry

submissions a month—sometimes more, sometimes less.

TDE: I assume you "bank" some amount of stories and poems for issues beyond what's currently in production. Do you pay authors on acceptance or when a piece is published?

EH: Yes, we do bank inventory, although not as much as you might think! Usually just an issue's worth. We pay upon acceptance.

TDE: In addition to the Writer's Guidelines posted on the websites are there any tips or advice you can add for fiction or poetry.

EH: When submitting to any magazine, it's really important to get a feel for what that magazine publishes. So pick up an issue, listen to our free podcast, and follow the authors that are already appearing in our pages. That is probably the best tip. For instance, if you read *Analog* you'll know there's no point sending any fantasy our way. We just don't publish it. There needs to be a kernel of science or technology at the core of an *Analog* tale.

One thing I always tell writers who are starting out is to seek out a writing community. Find a peer workshop; join a writing group. Our editors shouldn't be the first people seeing a manuscript. Stories and poems should be refined through revision and critique before being submitted. Personally, I know that my own writing is vastly improved by the feedback I receive from the workshops I belong to. Getting outside criticism is the best bet for getting work into publication shape.

Since I'm the poetry editor of the magazines, I can get a little more specific with my tips here. I like to see poems that make surprising imaginative leaps, use metaphor, symbolism, and imagery in new and inventive ways, and speak to the human (or extraterrestrial!) condition. *Analog* is particularly interested in science poetry. We of course publish science fiction poetry, but we also love science poetry without the SF aspect. *Asimov's* will publish it all—science fiction, fantasy, or science poetry.

TDE: Would you expand on the major and minor differences between today's *Asimov's* and *Analog*?

EH: The most striking difference is that all *Analog* stories must have a kernel of science or technology at their core, and the science used in these stories must be plausible. *Analog* doesn't publish any fantasy, or even science fiction where the science aspect seems like fantasy— unless there is a good reason for it that is explained in the story. To put it more simply, *Analog* will only publish hard science fiction. *Asimov's* publishes hard science fiction, soft science fiction, slipstream, weird fiction, and some fantasy.

On a more micro level, our departments are quite different. *Analog* includes at least one science fact article every issue, along with a nonfiction column by our resident physicist John G. Cramer titled "The Alternate View." He keeps us all up to date on exciting new discovers on the physics front. Something else particular to *Analog* is our "Brass Tacks" page, where we print letters from readers that might quibble over the science in a story or add interesting thoughts. *Asimov's* includes columns "On the Net" by James Patrick Kelly and "Reflections" by Robert Silverberg. These are nonfiction pieces that deal with science fiction culture online (James Patrick Kelly) and historic looks at early science fiction by Silverberg. Both magazines include a book review column.

TDE: You're the author of several chapbooks, including the recent *Space on Earth*. What's it about and how did it come together?

EH: *Space on Earth* is a short collection of poems with similar themes. I often write about new (or old!) discoveries in the solar system, galaxy, and universe. I find that astronomy is a natural metaphor for almost any human condition, and I enjoy juxtaposing the large relationships between celestial bodies and the small, sometimes petty relationships here on Earth. I also find myself drawn to ecological themes, and those can be found here in *Space on Earth* as well as my forthcoming book *Beach Vocabulary*.

The cover for *Space on Earth* was done by Samuel Hockaday, and it was published by Grey Book Press.

TDE: When is *Beach Vocabulary* due out?

EH: *Beach Vocabulary* doesn't have an exact publication date due to COVID-19 related delays. But I'm hoping it will be out in early 2021. It's coming out from Red Bird Chapbooks <redbirdchapbooks.com> and is a series of poems written about (or while staying on) Fire Island. Many of the poems are set in the National Park communities on the island—Watch Hill, Sunken Forest, and Talisman. I have a friend who works for the park service and have been fortunate enough to get first-hand details on the ecology there that made their way into the poems.

TDE: What is your writing process?

EH: My writing process definitely

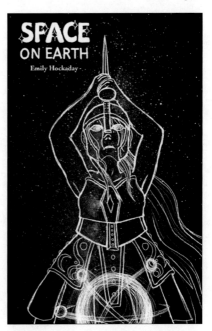

Space on Earth by Emily Hockaday, Grey Book Press, 2019. Cover by Samuel Hockaday.

varies. But here is a loose idea: I often participate in monthly "poem-a-day" groups in order to make sure I set aside quiet time each day (if only five minutes!) to let a poem surface. I find inspiration most frequently in my everyday life—nature, family, headlines, interactions with others. Like most writers, I sometimes get stuck—especially when I'm writing a poem every day—and in those cases I will dig out a writing prompt. That can be a really fruitful experience, as a writing prompt will usually provoke a poem that is totally different in tone or style or subject matter.

Once I have a batch of raw poems, I sort them by how much editing they need. The ones that are almost ready I'll polish and start sending out. Ones that need more work get set aside for workshop. I'm lucky to belong to a really wonderful workshop group

Woman Looking Out Window: Queens, New York

The New Horizons inches toward Pluto
and back here we wait

for data. Slower and slower
it comes. How much of this

is an accident? I fill my home
with plants and we trade breath;

decaying animals are broken
down by worms which are eaten

by birds some of which also eat
seeds and thus plant trees and berry bushes.

You know all this:
it has been tracked by graphs, charts,
and population curves. Looking out

at the night sky, I use an App
on my husband's smartphone

to point out when Mars
is under my feet, through the floor

or rising on the night horizon. I have used
my tiny brain

to try to look at this from an outside
vantage point. Will I get

another chance? Or was this the only life
not to screw up, and is it too late now? Are the pictures

coming further and further apart? Soon,
will there be no pictures at all?

—Emily Hockaday

Poem from *Space on Earth*. Image by Pexels from Pixabay.

that meets regularly and provides insightful feedback. Belonging to workshops and swapping writing has been invaluable to my craft.

After a poem is workshopped, I'll edit it, title it (That is almost always the last step—I hate titles!), and start sending it out for publication.

TDE: It's a challenge to stop tinkering with a story or an article. I'm guessing it's even more difficult with a poem since every single word is so important. How do you know when you're done?

EH: I don't ever really know! I start sending poems out if they feel ready or have gone through substantial edits, but sometimes I can't stop myself from editing them beyond. I'm especially likely to go back and tinker with a poem if it goes through several rounds of rejections. Even poems that have been published in journals aren't safe! I've been known to make revisions to poems after they've been published in a literary journal but before they come out in a chapbook.

TDE: You mentioned sending off poems. Where has your work been published?

EH: Some of my 2020 publications include poems in the *Poets of Queens* anthology, *Literary Mama*, *Coffin Bell*, Indolent Books, and *Middle House Review*. Over the years I've had work in a number of journals including *The North American Review*, *Spoon River Poetry Review*, and *Cosmonaut's Avenue*. I also have chapbooks from Finishing Line Press, Dancing Girl Press, Grey Book Press, and Zoo Cake Press.

TDE: Your author's website, <emilyhockaday.com>, states you're available for freelance projects. What freelance work

do you find most interesting?

EH: I enjoy editing and writing copy. I've taken on freelance projects ranging from fiction to hedge fund management articles.

TDE: Throughout 2020, the design and content of *Analog* paid tribute to its 90th year. How did readers respond? What's in store, in terms of look-and-feel for 2021?

EH: We've had a lot of readers writing in with memories associated with our retrospective reprint series—in which we had guest editors with an *Analog* connection choose a story from our history to showcase—as well as noting other stories from our past that have stayed with them.

Readers particularly liked the throw-back logo and cover design. Trevor and I thought those would be a hit. Many folks expressed interest in keeping that design moving forward, but we felt that would take some of the novelty away and make it less special, so readers can look forward to a new, modern cover design for 2021. And not to worry, our centennial will be here soon enough with the opportunity for another throw-back look!

TDE: 2020 has been a tough year. How has putting the magazines together changed during the pandemic?

EH: The biggest change is that now everything is done electronically. I have to admit that I miss editing on paper, though we are all getting used to doing it on the computer. Pre pandemic we edited the first drafts on paper and looked at the boards on paper. I do still print out the final PDFs before sending those off to the printer, but otherwise I do everything with Microsoft

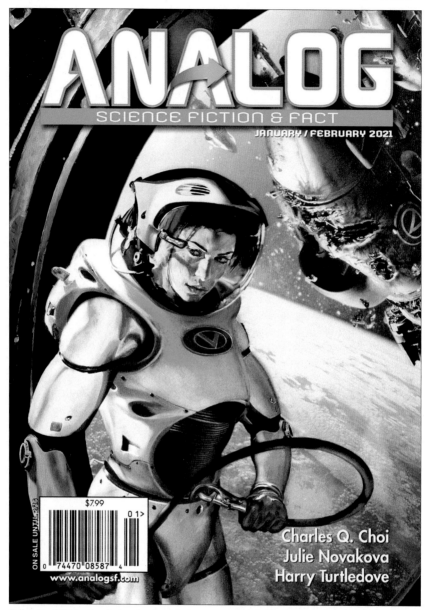

Following 2020's retro design *Analog* debuts a new masthead for its Jan/Feb 2021 edition.

Word or Adobe Reader at this point.

Another consequence of the pandemic is that the collaborative feel of editing is missing. If I come across something that I feel needs to be changed, I can no longer just hop over to Trevor or Sheila's office and hammer it out with them. Instead, we have to take notes and go back and forth over email, which is less efficient (and less satisfying). We do still have some phone and Zoom meetings, but I think one major downside to working at home every day is the loss of collaboration and easy communication.

TDE: These are challenging times for publishers. How are your magazines doing?

EH: This is one area of the magazines in which I am pretty uninformed—so apologies for not having more of an answer for you! But the basic gist is that digital and print subs are pretty similarly matched, and we believe there's been an uptick in sales in general (since the pandemic), as there has been for other Dell publications. A lot of folks are turning to literature for entertainment during these unprecedented times.

TDE: Tell us about your anthology with Jackie Sherbow, *Terror at the Crossroads*. Do you have other collections planned?

EH: *Terror at the Crossroads* is an ebook collection <barnesandnoble.com> of horror stories pulled from the four Dell digests—*Alfred Hitchcock's Mystery Magazine, Ellery Queen's Mystery Magazine, Asimov's Science Fiction Magazine*, and *Analog Science Fiction and Fact*. Jackie Sherbow chose stories from the two mystery magazines, and I picked pieces from the science fiction titles. We found ourselves trading stories over the years that we thought the other person would particularly enjoy—and lo and behold, they were always stories with a creepy horror vibe. We took it as a sign! It was a lot of fun working on this project with Jackie, and while we have no imminent plans for another collaboration, I really hope we can work together on other anthologies in the future.

TDE: You mentioned earlier managing *Analog* and *Asimov's* social media. What platforms are

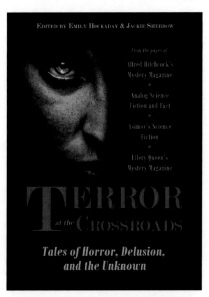

Terror at the Crossroads edited by Emily Hockaday and Jackie Sherbow Penny Publications, 2018.

you on, and how do you use each to complement the digests and expand their reach? How do readers respond to the various venues?

EH: We're on Twitter, Instagram, and Facebook, as well as having two companion blogs. The handle for *Analog* is @analog_sf and *Asimov's* is @asimovs_sf. The blogs are <TheAstoundingAnalogCompanion.com> and <FromEarthTotheStars.com>. We also have podcasts with Podomatic that stream on Spotify and iTunes. Once we stepped into social media, we went full steam ahead.

The blogs are great because they feature behind-the-scenes content from authors that a lot of readers find really fascinating. We do a lot of Q&As to learn more about the featured story and the author in general, and we also get fantastic guest posts from our authors on topics ranging from wormhole mathematics (Greg Egan, of course!) to Colombian science fiction (M.L. Clark).

We use Twitter, Facebook, and Instagram fairly similarly, in that we promote the blog posts, stories, podcasts, and authors with related images, story excerpts, author quotes, and art from the magazine. Instagram is very satisfying since it is so art-focused. We primarily use Instagram to showcase older covers, preview our upcoming covers, and display art or poetry from the magazines. Our most popular posts are sneak peek posts of upcoming issues, with our next most popular being throwback-Thursday or flashback-Friday posts. Our followers love the vintage covers (and so do I)!

TDE: Outside of the magazines, what's the best way for readers to keep up with your projects and interests?

EH: I'm on Twitter as @E_Hockaday, and I do update my personal website every now and then (though not as often as I should!). That is <emilyhockaday.com>.

Isaac Asimov's
Science Fiction Magazine
Davis Publications, Inc.
Vol. 1 No. 1 Spring 1977
Editorial Director: Isaac Asimov
Editor: George H Scithers
Associate Editor: Gardner Dozois
Art Director: Irving Bernstein
Producton Director: Carl Bartee
5.25" x 7.75" 192 pages
$1.00 cover price

Contents

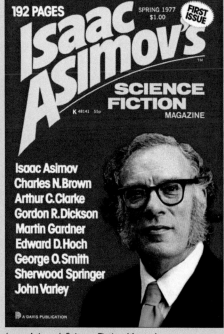

Isaac Asimov's Science Fiction Magazine
Vol. 1 No. 1 Spring 1977

Thanks to Clark Dissmeyer for this copy.

Sword & Sorcery Annual
Review by Richard Krauss

"The last fling Sol Cohen had with reprint magazines came in the winter of 1974/75 when he issued the nonfiction *U.F.O. Annual* and the *Sword & Sorcery Annual*. The latter had arisen because of the increase in sales in issues of *Fantastic*, which contained a new Conan story."
–*Science Fiction, Fantasy, and Weird Fiction Magazines*, Greenwood Press, 1985

Conan was a hot property in 1975. Editor/Publisher Sol Cohen purchased the reprint rights to "Queen of the Black Coast" and commissioned *Fantastic* regular Steve Fabian for a cover. The balance of the one-shot *Sword & Sorcery Annual* is filled with an excellent selection of supernatural sagas pulled from the *Fantastic* vault.

To streamline production, the reprints were literally pulled directly from their sources. The Conan pages were typeset in a single column for *Avon Fantasy Reader* No. 8 (Nov. 1948)—and if it was good enough then, it was good enough for 1975. The only difference is the addition of a series of one-inch circular illos by Fabian to adorn the poems that open each of the story's five chapters. Fabian also provided a full page illustration for the inside front cover.

The balance of the book is presented in two-column layout pulled from back issues of *Fantastic*, along with their illustrations, and all the original typos—plus a nonfiction piece from *Amazing*.

Queen of the Black Coast
by Robert E. Howard

This early Conan adventure was originally the cover story for *Weird Tales* May 1934, and later on *Avon Fantasy Reader* No. 8, Nov. 1948. It's wonderful to see three different artists' interpretations of the story, including the cover and inside front cover of *S&S* by Steve Fabian.

Wikipedia states Howard was paid $115 by *Weird Tales* in 1934—$2,238 in today's dollars. The story remains a favorite of Howard's fans.

As the story opens, Conan is on horseback, hightailing it out of Argos, with a posse not far enough behind. His stallion thunders to a stop at the end of a pier. With nowhere else to go, he leaps squarely

Fantastic Stories Special—1975

SWORD & SORCERY annual

75¢   08289   ICD

Thrilling adventures of CONAN THE CIMMERIAN

QUEEN OF THE BLACK COAST
by Robert E. Howard

**L. SPRAGUE DE CAMP:
SWORD and SATIRE**
by Sam Moskowitz

THE PILLARS OF CHAMBALOR
by John Jakes

HORSEMAN
by Roger Zelazny

MASTER OF CHAOS
by Michael Moorcock

THE CLOUD OF HATE
by Fritz Leiber

**THE MIRROR
OF CAGLIASTRO**
by Robert Arthur

THE MASTERS
by Ursula K. Leguin

onto the deck of a galley, demanding the ship get underway immediately. Tito, the ship's master, who suffers no fondness for the courts of Argos, nor its swordsmen, orders his crew to depart at once.

The ship is bound for Kush, and soon beyond the range of the arrows

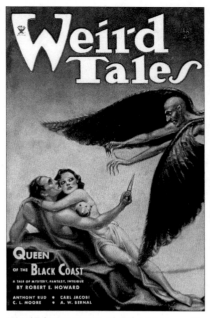

Weird Tales May 1934 with Robert E. Howard's "Queen of the Black Coast." Cover by Margaret Brundage.

Avon Fantasy Reader No. 8 1948 with Robert E. Howard's "Queen of the Black Coast." Cover by Manuel Isip(?).

of Conan's jurors. The oarsmen take them past the city of Shem, past the broad bay where the Styx river empties into the ocean, and then the southern borders of Stygia.

"So they beat southward, and master Tito began to look for the high-walled villages of the black people. But they found only smoking ruins on the shore of a bay, littered with naked black bodies."

The work of pirates, likely led by Bêlit, a Shemite woman whose black raiders have sent many good tradesmen like Tito and crew to their graves.

At sunrise, a lookout shouts warning. A slender serpentine galley, driven by forty oars on either side, powers its way toward them. The tradesmen double their strokes in vain as the gap between the two vessels continues to narrow. Before the pirates are upon them, Conan takes command.

"'Up, lads!' he roared, loosing with a vicious twang of cord. 'Grab your steel and give these dogs a few knocks before they cut our throats! Useless to bend your backs any more: they'll board us ere we can row another fifty paces!'"

Sadly, the muscular oarsmen are no match for the pirates' arrows, spears, and fighting prowess. Tito's crew rapidly dwindles in defeat, with Conan alone pressing the enemy back, then boarding the pirate vessel to wreak havoc on their superior numbers.

It is the pirates' mistress who abruptly ends the battle. "Bêlit sprang before the blacks, beating down their spears. She turned toward Conan, her bosom heaving, her eyes flashing. Fierce fingers of wonder caught at his heart." And she is no less awestruck with him.

With Tito and his crew dead and dying, their ship already taking water, Conan succumbs to the charms of his new queen while her pirates loot the merchant ship before it disappears below roiling waters.

Their new allegiance bound in passion, Conan, Bêlit, and galley crew sail along the southern coast till they reach the mouth of a sullen river.

"'This is the river Zarkheba, which is Death,' said Bêlit. 'Its waters are poisonous. See how dark and murky they run? Only venomous reptiles live in that river. The black people shun it. Once a Stygian galley, fleeing from me, fled up the river and vanished. I anchored in this very spot, and days later, the galley came floating down the dark waters, its decks blood-stained and deserted. Only one man was on board, and he was mad and died gibbering. The cargo was intact, but the crew had vanished into silence and mystery.'"

Tales of great treasure entice the fearless pair as they cast their fate down the dark river toward an adventure of unimagined wealth and danger. A classic Conan saga, worth reading again and again.

L. Sprague de Camp: Sword and Satire by Sam Moskowitz

The digest's only nonfiction piece, from *Amazing Stories* Feb. 1964, provides a brief biography of de Camp's early life, followed by an excellent, more detailed look at his career and collaborations.

The Pillars of Chambalor
by John Jakes

By 1975, Brak the Barbarian was

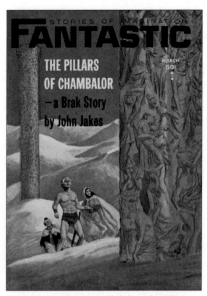

Fantastic March 1965 with John Jakes'"The Pillars of Chambalor." Cover by Gray Morrow.

the star of three novels on bookstore racks, so this reprint from *Fantastic* March 1965, along with its full-page illustration by Gray Morrow, was prime for inclusion here. Brak wakes in the desert beneath a searing red sun. His groggy wits slowly clear as he recalls a sudden sandstorm that nearly killed him, and as he soon discovers, finished his pony. The inn where he last spoke to another man, was built with a large court to accommodate caravans, and had warned him of an ancient city in the desert, Chambalor. Climbing the crest of a high dune, he spots twin rows of giant columns towering above what once were stately avenues.

"And while the big barbarian could not make out precisely what was carven upon their stone surfaces, the dimly-seen decorations lent the pillars a curious shifting look, as though the stones were subtly alive."

Brak scratches his forearm across

Fantastic May 1964 with Michael Moorcock's "Master of Chaos." Cover by Ed Emshwiller.

his eyes and when he looks again, spots the figure of a man trudging through the sand. Driven by hunger and thirst, he rushes down the dune, kicking at a blue-veined basalt slab buried in the sand.

"He had taken two more steps when ghastly, stinging pain seared his left leg." The feeler of a giant spider-like monstrosity had him in its grasp.

He draws his broadsword, but the pain saps the barbarian's strength. Sawing at the feeler has no effect. With a mighty swing, he finally severs the feeler in a single blow. The wounded creature retreats as the once mighty warrior staggers in the soft sand and finally collapses in a heap.

The sound of voices seeps into Brak's consciousness. He rises on an elbow and sees the traveler he'd spotted earlier, an old man, and a young woman. The man is Zama Khan, the woman, his daughter,

Dareet. The poison left from the sand-spider is slowly killing the barbarian, but the clever Zama Khan can save him—for a price.

Khan aims to uncover the treasures of Chambalor and needs the strength of a powerful warrior to open the massive stone doors that protect it. If Brak agrees to help him, the wizard will prepare a poultice to reverse the effects of the venom.

Of course, he agrees. And when Brak's strength returns, he follows Zama and Dereet into the bowels of Chambalor, where the trio find far more than they traded for.

Jakes conceived of his barbarian hero knowing when Robert E. Howard died, there would be no more Conan tales—hence Jakes invented Brak and wrote more adventures himself.

Master of Chaos
by Michael Moorcock

Queen Eloarde commands her consort, Earl Aubec of Malador, conqueror of all the Southern nations, to add the Kaneloon to her kingdom. The enigmatic castle stands at the very edge of the World's End, beyond which only the swirling, shifting sea of Chaos exists.

The mighty swordsman preferred the arms of his Queen, but he must do as he is bidden and with some reluctance make his way to the foreboding castle and its rumored recluse the Dark Lady.

Climbing the twisting path that leads Aubec ever higher, he at last reaches the castle and chooses one of several dark doorways that bid him enter. A chill descends immediately as the warrior finds himself lost in a labyrinth of snaking corridors.

"The madness lurking in the

depths of his brain filtered out and became fear and, immediately following the sensation of fear, came the shapes. Swift-moving shapes darting from several directions, gibbering, fiendish, utterly horrible."

As the creatures grow bolder, Aubec attacks them, slashing and driving them back with his massive broadsword. Yet for every retreat, the creatures return, giving him little time to rest and regain his waning strength. It is during a brief respite that he realizes the creatures resume in response to his fears. They are but phantoms, manifest through a sorcerer's trick of the mind. With valiant resolve, Aubec calms his ragged nerves and as he relaxes, the creatures and the walls of the labyrinth dissolve.

But there is no time for rest. Aubec's quest is only beginning. He will face a giant metallic golem and the Dark Lady sorceress, Micella, before he meets his fate within the swirling mysteries of Chaos.

Adorned with an illustration by the great Virgil Finlay, this Earl Aubec of Malador adventure was a one-off sword and sorcery yarn by the creator of Elric of Melniboné, an albino antihero featured in fiction, games, comics, music, and film.

The Mirror of Cagliostro
by Robert Arthur

Misspelled "Cagliastro" on the cover and contents page, this engaging creeper by the cocreator of the Mysterious Traveler, leaves its broadswords to the barbarians in favor of straight sorcery.

The murderous Cagliostro swaps souls with his victims, trapping them behind the glass of an indestructible mirror while he inhabits their

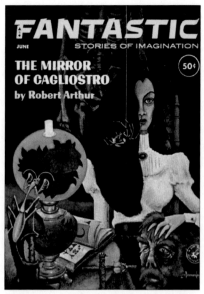

Fantastic June 1963 with Robert Arthur's "The Mirror of Cagliostro." Cover by Lee Brown Coye.

bodies to continue his serial-murdering mayhem through the ages.

Our first brush with the villain, circa 1910, occurs in London as we bear witness to the death by strangulation of one Molly Blanchard at the inhabited hands of Charles, Duke of Burchester. In these early days, the sorcerer is surely wicked, but not yet clever. Retiring to the Burchester mansion, it takes merely an hour before Scotland Yard is literally knocking at the door of his second story studio. Knowing only one escape, "Charles, Duke of Burchester, flung himself from the casement window and jellied himself on the cobblestones below."

Fast forward to Paris, 1963, where we find Harry Langham, associate professor of history at Boston College, engaged in research for his doctoral thesis on, of all things, the mysterious Count Cagliostro. Professor Henri Thibaut, curator of the Musée des Antiq-

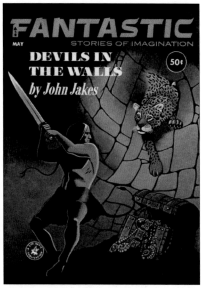

Fantastic May 1963 with Fritz Leiber's "The Cloud of Hate." Cover by Vernon Kramer.

uités Historique, warns Langham of the dangers of such pursuit, yet imparts him with two leads in hopes they will dissuade him.

The first is the tomb of Yvette Dulaine, deep in the catacombs of the Church of St. Martin. Interred in 1780, the church's caretaker leads Langham through its subterranean crypts until at last they stand before a plain, stone tomb, topped with a stone slab. The caretaker slides the lid aside and Langham cannot believe what lies before him. The ancient body is so perfectly preserved he's convinced it's made of wax.

When questioned, the caretaker replies, "She is not dead. Yet she is not alive. She exists in some dark dimension it is not well to think of. The Count Cagliostro took his revenge on her. She will sleep thus, until the very stones of Paris become dust around her."

Still struggling with this paradox, Langham proceeds to the second

lead, a dingy, second-hand shop in the Soho district in London. There he finds a tall, hinged mirror of oval pier glass. A mirror of unbreakable glass, its surface painted black to deny a reflection. But Langham notices a spot at the bottom where the paint had chipped away. He stoops to his knees and peers into the reflection, but the face he sees is not his own. It is the reflection of Yvette Delaine, mouthing the words, "Sauvez-moi!" Save me!

The encounter transforms Langham. He ships the mirror from London to Boston and begins the task of removing the paint from its surface. When it's done, he finds his worst fears realized as he's swept up in Cagliostro's sorcery and must use every ability he can muster to survive the ordeal.

Running 30 pages, including three with illustrations by Dan Adkins, "Cagliostro" is this digest's longest story.

The Cloud of Hate by Fritz Leiber

A swashbuckling fantasy by the man credited with coining the descriptor "sword and sorcery" is both welcome and wholly appropriate for this digest. The tale, with artwork by Leo R. Summers, alternates between a growing threat and the watchful pair, Fafhrd and the Gray Mouser, as they trade gibes, and lament their lack of riches.

The threat is borne from the Hall of Hate, where the combined psyche of its aggrieved worshippers manifests in swirling ribbons of fog that pour through the Hall's window slits to ravage the streets of Lankhmar. Forming a serpent-like fog, the collective ire seeks the worst of the city's thieves and

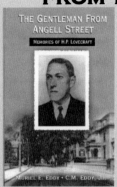

The Village of the Wraith

A tale of sword & sorcery by Richard Krauss
Illustrations by Rick McCollum

Then he saw her. A ghostly wraith, slipping into his field of vision, cloaked in the folds of a dark burnoose.

Sometime after midnight, while much of the farming village of Aldwier lay in tense slumber, ready to bolt upright at the slightest rustle of brittlebush outside an open window—or worse, a sleeping child awakened by a wrinkled hand smothering its scream, she silently struck. On this night, it was Cartus, a ten-year-old male, taken just like the others.

In the end, there had been nothing different. All the preparations the parents, the farmhands, and the elders had made were useless. The mother of Cartus, Vessa, had retired to her bed with the boy beside her, while the father, Walid, stood watch outside their sleeping quarter's window. A precaution repeated at every house and hovel throughout the small village. Every household

held vigil. Those without offspring kept watch over the fields and livestock. Yet, the result was the same as every other sorrowful morning.

Walid had idled his time counting and connecting stars in the clear night sky. The air was still, and the cool, moonless night granted welcome relief from the day's broiling heat. The throaty rumble of a wisent or bison in some far off meadow was answered by a chorus of dogs defending their masters' imagined threat. Walid yawned, his mind wandered. As if dreaming, he realized a presence seeping into his mind. He tried to turn his gaze but found his muscles unresponsive. Suddenly alert, he tried to raise his arms to blow the horn clutched at his side, but it remained frozen in his grasp. He tried to cry out in alarm, but

his lips were silenced, not even the anguished moan he felt crashing against his hopes could be heard.

Then he saw her. A ghostly wraith, slipping into his field of vision, cloaked in the folds of a dark burnoose. Her skin, what little was visible, was pale, nearly white, and seemed to emit a faint phosphorescence that obscured her features. She floated in utter silence. Not even a rustle came from the heavy fabric she wore as she drifted through the open window and merged with the darkness inside his home.

Walid felt his heart bursting, but even he could not hear the rabid surge of blood against his ear drums. He was as if dead, yet still alive to watch in helpless horror as the wraith reappeared, now with his son, Cartus, mingled in the folds of her cloak. How had the sorceress stolen the boy without awakening Vessa? Had the crone slashed the throat of his poor wife as she slept? Anguish drowned his fractured mind as the life he knew slipped away from his ken.

Yet the night suffered on, as if it would never end. Walid remained frozen, his mind tortured by his helplessness and the hopelessness of his plight. He wept in great waves of sorrow, motionless and silent until the first rays of sunlight filtered through the branches of the dry forest that surrounded Aldwier, washed over him, and lifted the spell. He collapsed to the ground in exhaustion.

But he knew he could not rest, and managed to bring the wisent horn, still clutched in his fingers, to his parched lips to blow out a low blast of alarm to the village. A farmhand appeared at the gate of a nearby pen and came running when he saw Walid laid out in the dust.

It wasn't long before the night's sorrow spread across the village. To Walid's relief, Vessa was unharmed, a victim of the same spell that had rendered him helpless. Once daylight broke, she too regained her movement and her tongue. But she had not suffered as Walid, for the paralysis had shackled her before she woke. She could add nothing to shed further light on the abduction.

In another world, the Royan upon which the Helg priest rode might well be described as a long-haired dray horse. The powerful beast was more suited to the plow than bearing a man across the ruts between Aldwier and Ontair. The elders had sent the priest to the city to seek the help of one whose ilk dwelt in the alehouses of Ontair: a mercenary.

The twisted road was rugged and the going slow. By all rights what should have been an hour's journey took twice as long in part thanks to the brittlebush obscuring the path and the ancient knellwood tree roots knotting the ground. The Royan stumbled more than once, but Perth allowed his mount to set the pace, for he knew it better to ride than lead a lame beast behind him should he push the dray too hard. The day was hot and Perth cursed himself for not having left at dawn before the heat burnt down from another day of cloudless skies. Although never a drinking man at heart, he felt he might welcome the froth of a cold mead when he reached Waylan's alehouse in Ontair.

The hiss of bowhorn beetles chattered in the dry air. High

above, silhouetted in the sky, a dark scavenger circled in patient arcs, waiting for some poor soul to surrender to the heat. Not today, thought Perth, for his journey was not so dire, and presently he spied the roof of a farmhouse over a clump of twisted thorns. He wiped his brow and sighed, anticipating the welcome shade inside Waylan's house of ale. Soon the dirt road smoothed out and in another mile the Royan joined a main road Perth knew led to the center of Ontair.

When he spotted Waylan's on his right, Perth guided the dray horse past toward a two-story stable, where he dismounted.

"Welcome," said the young stableboy emerging from the shadows of the barn. "How may the stables of Durwall be of service?"

"I am Perth. Water, then a shady stall with feed for my mount. And a good combing to clear his matt, whence he's properly cooled. I shall bide my time in the alehouse yonder whilst he rests for our journey home to Aldwier. We'll leave well before the sunset."

"I'll take good care of your Royan, Perth," said the lad. "He'll be ready for your journey in two hours time."

"Will two coppers cover your troubles?"

"Indeed it will. Enjoy your drink. It's said that Waylan serves Ontair's finest amber mead."

Perth gave the lad his shiny coppers and handed off the Royan's reins. He gave the dray a pat on its hindquarters, turned away, and strode into Waylan's alehouse.

The heat shed a level or two the moment he was inside. Blinded by its relative darkness, Perth stood rooted inside the door as his eyes adjusted to the dim. The smell of ferments and hemp washed over him as the mummer of conversation settled on his ears. Slowly the shape of tables and chairs emerged in the foreground and a long, lacquered bar formed through the aleroom's smokey haze.

As soon as he could see his way, Perth strode to the bar where he was greeted by the barman, a man with wild, umber hair covering his head and face. His dark eyes were bright, and he spoke through a toothy smile, "As you are a man not yet known to me, I venture you have newly arrived in our fair city. I will serve you at your pleasure, but may I suggest a hearty mug of dark amber mead?"

"I am Perth," said the priest. "A stranger no more."

"And as you've likely guessed, I am Waylan. I am pleased to serve you." The barman gave a slight nod and turned to fetch a draught.

Perth settled onto a stool at the bar as Waylan brought a tankard of amber mead topped with a frothy head. Before Perth could take his first taste, he was flanked by two ragged looking fellows, one at each of the stools beside him. The man on his right, a lanky fellow with a dirty face, ran his eyes over Perth and reached out for the sigil suspended from his neck.

"Helgan, eh?" he said as he let the medallion flop back against Perth's chest.

"Helgan priest," said Perth.

"Well, no priest I ever heard of drank mead. What brings you here?"

Waylan broke in. "Give the man his idle, Dez. Can't you see he's barely dusted off the road before you set in to your cure your boredom."

"Give off, Waylan. I'm no
bother to the man. I am, priest?
My chum, Goft here, and I don't
see strangers oft, so we're interested to know how you happened
this way, and what it is you seek."

"I thank you for your steady
hand, Waylan," said Perth. "But I
have no secrets, and you, friend
Dez, proved yourself a percep-
tive man. Perhaps you and your
chum Goft can help me."

Dez closed his eyes and nodded
thrice as a satisfied smirk cut across
his stubbled mug. "I knew it! Any
priest worth his creed is always on
the take. So, let's have it, vicar."

Perth took a breath and managed a weak smile. "I come from
Aldwier, your neighbor to the north.
Several children have been taken
from our village, abducted by some
ghostly visage that appears whilst
we sleep. It bewitches our watch-
men, freezing them in silence, as
if cast in stone, until the light of
dawn frees them from the spell."

Goft's pea green tunic was as
weathered as his dried skin and as
battered as his tangle of hair. He'd
remained disinterested in Perth until
this moment, when he snatched the
priest's tankage from the bar and
downed a third of its contents in a
single gulp, as Waylan, too late to
intervene, sneered disapproval.

Perth let the rude behavior
slide and continued his plea. "Our
council of elders has sent me to
enlist the aid of a warrior to find the
wraith and return our children."

"And what makes you
think they're still among
the living?" said Dez.

"Only hope, I'm afraid. That,
and they were taken alive."

"Taken as slaves, no doubt."

Perth sighed. "The village of
Aldwier has taken a collection,
gathering all our stocks. We will
pay a bounty of 47 golds to the
man or men who can help us. The
reward will be paid upon the return
of our children, with proof the
wraith is powerless to retaliate."

"That's a tempting reward,"
said Dez, showing a mouthful of
stained teeth. "We just might be
able to help you out. But it sounds
dangerous. We'd need the gold
upfront to take such a risk."

"I've been authorized to pay a
fee of ten golds upfront, but first
I must be convinced your inten-
tions are true and your skills are up
to the task. It will be dangerous."

Dez sprang from his stool and
snatched the strap of Perth's satchel
from his shoulder. The coins inside it
jingled. As Perth and Dez each tried
to wrench the bag free from the other, Dez tried to justify his actions: "I
need proof, you can pay that much."

Waylan moved to intervene, but
Goft reached over the bar, palmed
the barman's face, and shoved
him backward. Caught off balance, Waylan faltered against the
counter behind him and skidded
down to the floor. Goft immediately grabbed the collar of Perth's
tunic from behind and yanked it
tightly around the priest's throat.

Choking and outnumbered,
Perth's fingers released his grip on
his satchel as Dez snatched it away.

An angry bellow erupted from a
corner of the alehouse, "Enough!"

All three turned to see a massive
brute lunge toward them, his wild,
black mane trailing in his wake. A
powerful hand clenched the tunic
Dez wore, lifting the thug off his

feet, and slammed his head into Goft's. Both thugs crashed to the floor as Perth adjusted his collar and stooped to retrieve his satchel.

The brute towered over the thugs as they scrambled to find their feet. "Leave now," he growled. The two thieves backed away, bumping into chairs until they reached the door and left without taking their eyes off the massive stranger.

When Perth and Waylan reclaimed their composure, the barman was first to speak. "My apologies, friends. Dez and Goft can be a surly lot. Too much time on their hands, I think. Unfortunately, they sometimes make trouble. We're lucky Kragar here was close at hand and willing to stop their assault."

Perth nodded and gave Kragar an appraising look. Bare to the waist, the stranger seemed to be made of muscle. He too wore a medallion around his thick neck, and the sheath at his waist held a skinning knife the size of a man's forearm. "Thank you for routing those troublemakers, Kragar. My name is Perth. You may be just the man I'm looking for."

"I claim no benevolence," said Kragar, "your bounty seems a fair price for your task."

"May I take it, you're interested?"

"Your wraith sounds like a sorceress; perhaps a mere crone. Where do I find her?"

"A prudent question. The sage, Doyen, leader of our council, has told me that our champion must first visit the seer, Zeya. Only she can tell you where to find this sorceress— and provide the wisdom to defeat her. Zeya dwells amid the dry forest, not far off the road that leads back to Aldwier. But, I must caution you, the task is perilous. We can not aid you. tis a battle you must fight alone."

"I accept your challenge, Helgan priest of Aldwier," said Kragar and offered his hand.

The priest took it and placed ten gold coins therein. "Thank you, friend Kragar. We shall leave immediately."

The Royan was duly rested and watered when Perth and Kragar retrieved their mounts to begin their trek toward Aldwier. Perth led the way, with Kragar astride a burly stallion of smooth, chestnut coat. The well-trod path was narrow, so they traveled one behind the other over the rutted, dusty ground. The better part of an hour passed without discussion under the broiling stare of the sun. When they reached a pair of giant knellwoods, their prickly branches crisscrossed above the path, Perth guided the Royan off the trail. He extracted a small wooden box from his satchel and handed it to Kragar.

The warrior opened the lid to reveal a compass.

"Your journey begins here," said Perth. "Look closely and you can see the path forks here. Follow this route to Zeya's sanctum. I'm told it isn't far, but follow the compass to stay northeast, should the path become unclear. She lives in a burrow below a mound of boulders. Tell her you serve Doyen and she will help you.

"May the gods protect you from the magik of them who would oppose your noble endeavor. I will continue on the main road to Aldwier to await your sweet success."

The two men grasped each other's forearms in farewell, then turned their mounts to-

The heads of two more serpents appeared above the rocks, and all three rushed toward their victim.

Kragar swung his blade, but the clever reptiles evaded its edge and two of them closed in, wrapping themselves around his legs. Kragar snatched their necks, one in each hand as his sword clanged onto the rocks beside him.

The remaining serpent slithered forward. Kragar raised his leg in an attempt to stomp on the reptile's head, but his foot crashed onto stone as the viper coiled and struck, sinking its fangs deep into his calf, injecting a cloudy serum into the warrior's blood stream.

Kragar reeled, his head dizzy, his vision blurred. The serpent withdrew. Kragar's grip on the others loosened, allowing them to wriggle free, and disappear into the rocks. "Do not fear death, mighty warrior," a voice inside his head advised him. "Zeya's sting is not deadly."

As a cloud of darkness engulfed him, Kragar felt as if a deep, paralyzing sleep had gripped him, yet his mind retained a gauzy consciousness. As he tried to gain his bearings, an image began to form through clouded vision. A narrow aperture broke in the rocky landscape, beckoning him to enter. He squeezed his bulk through the opening, as the passageway beyond widened. He followed its route twenty-paces, twisting downward until it opened into a cavern-like room built of massive timber posts and beams, with carefully fitted boulders making up its walls.

The air was cool, the space lit in candlelight. An ancient woman sat on a low bench before the mirror-like surface of a pool. The seer raised

ward their separate paths.

As Kragar guided his stallion off the main road, the knellwood grew thicker, providing a modicum of shade. He picked his way between them carefully, sometimes ducking to avoid the needles that shunned heat more effectively than leaves. He paused on occasion to refer to the compass. In what seemed half an hour, he came to a knoll of massive boulders. Kragar dismounted and tied the stallion's reins to a tree branch in a shady spot.

He strode along the perimeter of the boulders, carefully examining each rock for a sign. When he arrived at the base of a massive specimen, half buried in the ground, he paused. Perhaps it was a marker. Kragar climbed onto the pile.

Suddenly, the scaly head of a serpent thrust its head from between two boulders with a shrill hiss. Kragar stepped back and unleashed his broadsword from the scabbard fastened between his shoulders. The sibilant whisper was not a warning, but a call to its brothers.

her head as Kragar entered her sanctum. "Welcome, traveler," she said.

Kragar crept closer, grasping for his broadsword, but it was gone. He growled at the seer, "What spell have you cast upon me, woman? How did you bring me here, and where is my weapon?"

The seer's eyes narrowed as she drew in a breath. "I am Zeya. Did you not seek to find me and hear my counsel?" She paused to let the words settle into the mind of the dazed, nettled barbarian. "Before all else, you must tell me who sent you to me."

Kragar nodded, "I have made a pact with the Helg priest of Aldwier, Perth, he sent me here upon the advice of a wise man called Doyen. I am a warrior, known as Kragar. What is this place and what have you done with my broadsword?"

"Be patient, friend Kragar. All will be revealed to you shortly. I am not the woman you think you see before you. I am but a vision, enabled by the serum flowing from my lips into your veins. Its effects are transient, but necessary, or we could not converse.

"A short while ago, the head counsel of the elders of Aldwier— this Doyen you speak of—told me a warrior would come. A warrior hired to defeat the sorceress, Aneurin, and to return to their homes, the children she has enslaved."

"Aye," said Kragar. "I seek your guidance on where to find this crone and how to defeat her."

A faint smile curled the edges of Zeya's mouth. She sat silently as a low hum came from her lips and she closed her eyes, rocking back and forth in a slow, rhythmic motion. Time seemed to fade. A slow dawning came to Kragar, like a dream within a dreamworld. His peripheral vision faded, his attention drawn to the pool before them, its still waters darkening from clear to blackest night.

Then, upon its surface, an image formed. As if from a great height, looking down upon the village of Aldwier, its image slowly growing smaller as the vantage slid to the north and also to the west. The image panned until it settled on the Twill-Arn Forest, northwest of Aldwier, beneath the foothills of the Bremmen Range. The vantage shifted to a closer view above the scarid spruce until a dozen or more log houses were visible interspersed between the trees. Then the vision faded and pool returned to crystal clear, revealing its stony bottom once more.

Zeya's humming quieted and the slits of her eyes opened. "Now you have seen for yourself the answer to your first question—the lair of Aneurin. But beware, she is building a village. Each house, constructed by her army of slaves, are cut from the forest's spruce. Each house, the same. Each one empty, save for the sorceress herself, who wakes in a different dwelling each dawn, making it impossible for her enemies to detect her, before she finds them first."

"Why does the crone enslave only children? Surely, the farmers and their hands would make more suitable slaves."

"I cannot tell for certain," said Zeya. "I suspect Aneurin's magik has its limits. Her spells are strong enough to bind the will of men to her biding for short durations, but I suspect she secures more permanent results with children.

Perhaps their youth makes them less able to resist. It is also possible she deadens their wills with potions once they are within her grasp. Still, you must be wary of her powers."

"I will not depend on stealth to defeat her," said Kragar. "Tell me now of her weakness, the means by which she can be destroyed."

Zeya smiled and pressed the palms of her hands together. "Do not judge a sorceress by her stature. Never underestimate her power. However, like most of the elderwitches of Wellwood, Aneurin does have a weakness. It is her secret name. Say it aloud in her presence. Like a talisman, it will make her magik against you useless. She will become an ordinary woman for as long as she remains in your presence."

"And how does one learn her secret name?"

Zeya frowned. "Alas, that I cannot tell you. You must be clever and trick her into revealing it."

Upon regaining his broadsword from the rocks, Kragar lost no time making his way back to the main road and then onward to Aldwier. Upon his arrival, he met with Perth and the elder Doyen, who outfit him with three days of food and water and gave him their blessings for success. He struck out early the following day, before the first rays of sunlight bathed the tree tops of the knellwood forest and the songs of scrub wrens and verdin welcomed the morning.

He consulted the compass as Perth had instructed, and wove his way through the woods, slowly picking his way over the dry terrain. On the first night he slept above the Tarquin River that marked the end of a long day's ride for both horse and rider. As best the mercenary could tell, they had traveled three-quarters of the distance to the village of Aneurin. The knellwoods had given way to spruce as the terrain graded gently higher. Kragar ate a meal of bread and dried tack, his stallion, the coarse grasses that found footholds beneath the umbrella of spruce. Both drank the clear, cool waters of the Tarquin.

Well rested, Kragar rose at dawn to continue his journey to Aneurin. By late morning he felt as if the crone must be within striking distance. He found a tall spruce and scaled it, but found he had drifted to the north. In the distance he glimpsed what appeared to be several houses built of logs, like the ones he'd seen in Zeya's vision pool. He wondered if Aneurin could sense his presence, but dismissed such thoughts, knowing they mattered not. He would continue regardless.

Nearly an hour later, as Kragan approached Aneurin's settlement, he found a shady spot, well hidden from view and tied his mount to a sturdy branch. As he crept closer on foot, the sounds of building met his ears. Hammers pounding, axes and saws shaping timber, and the mesh of gears driving an auger. A muted voice cut through the hum of construction, high-pitched, but leaden and indistinct. A dozen children, he reckoned seven to fifteen years of age, were building log houses. They only spoke to give, or acknowledge directions, their faces stoic, eyes dull, as they toiled on the crone's behalf.

Kragar circled around, taking care none of the children would spot him. He peered into the

windows of each cabin he encountered. All empty. When he'd
finished the outermost, he crept
inside their perimeter and began
searching the settlement's interior.

He stopped counting the empty
houses he'd checked, and would've
lost his bearing if not for the scarid
spruce trees he'd marked by ar-
ranging stones beside their trunks.
At the next house, a blanket lay on
the wooden floor. Kragar's muscles
tensed and he reached over his
shoulder to draw his broadsword.

"Welcome," a graveled voice
spoke from behind the warrior.

Kragar turned to find the
sorceress Aneurin floating in
the air, just beyond the reach of
his sword. She flicked open her
hand and Krager's arms fell to his
sides, his sword dropping onto the
ground. He tried to move, but his
muscles no longer responded.

The witch drew closer and
brushed her fingers across his
mouth. "Now you can speak, fool.
Tell me why you have come here?"

Only Kragar's tongue
and lips were freed. "I have
come to slay you, crone!"

Aneurin cackled. "You cannot move and yet you think
you can threaten me? You are
truly simple-minded. But I am
not an unreasonable woman. I
will give you a test. If you pass, I
will send you on your way, with
your pledge never to return. But
if you fail, you will serve me for
the rest of your miserable life."

The witch brushed her
hand over Kragar's eyes and
blackness engulfed him.

"Stampede!" a dis-
tant voice yelled.

Kragar found himself astride his
stallion, galloping toward a massive
cloud of dust amid the thunder-
ing hoofs of bison. The herd was
panicked, racing across an open
plain toward a forest and the village
it sheltered. If the herd continued
their stampede, they'd likely trample
the village and all that lived there.

Kragar spurred his stallion
on, weaving his way through the
herd. At its head, a great brown
bison led the pack. Kragar's mount
hurtled through the dust and
spray of hooves, passing a dozen
of the great beasts. Kragar urged
his stallion on. Around him, the
bison snorted in gasps of breath
as they rumbled forward.

Krager held onto the stallion with one hand as the powerful steed neared the lead bison.
His horse nearly stumbled as it
brushed against the side of the
beast. Kragar leapt from his mount
onto the back of the great bull.
But the beast's hair was too short
for a hand hold. Kragar lunged
toward the bison's head, grabbing
onto its horns, one in each hand.
The annoyance caused the beast to
slow its frantic pace, as it tried to
shake off its unwelcome intruder.

But Kragar was too strong. The
muscles of his arms strained as he
slowly forced the head of the beast
to turn, its massive body following.
The beast was angry but exhausted
from running. As it slowed, the
herd followed suit. Kragar's stallion kept pace, but also kept its
distance from the larger animal.

The threat to the village had
been averted. Now Kragar would
have to escape the bull's ire and the
herd's crushing feet. He pulled up
on the beast's horns, forcing its head

back. It slowed, then answered his
attack by shaking its head, trying
to tear the warrior's grip free.

Barely able to hold on, Kragar
whistled to his steed and the
horse lunged sideways abreast
the bison. On the next thrust of
the bull's head, Kragar allowed
the force to propel his leap off
its shoulders and onto the back
of his stallion. Almost before he
settled, the great horse veered off
to the side and headed away from
the herd, toward the village.

As Kragar turned to look over
his shoulder at the herd, his strength
drained from his body and he
felt himself falling to the ground
as blackness swallowed him.

The ache in his shoulders
brought consciousness back to
Kragar. His arms were spread, his
wrists shackled at shoulder height
to the wall at his back. Although
he'd passed Aneurin's test, she'd
lied about freeing him. He found
his footing and raised himself to
stand, relieving the burden of his
weight from his shoulders, eyeing
the heavy straps around his wrists
holding him securely to the wall.

He was in a dungeon of sorts
with stone walls all round, tethered
like a beast. The air was damp and
fetid. The only hint of light, a faint
glow from somewhere beyond his
view. The mumbling beside him
came from an old woman, strapped
as Kragar. The chin of her weathered
face rested on her chest. The dingy
rags she wore covered her torso
down to her knees. Her feet were
bare and stained from the wet spot
in which she stood. The buzzing of
insects only made her plight worse.

No longer frozen, Kragar

strained against his bonds, but they
did not budge. His broadsword
and skinning knife were gone. He
licked his parched lips and spoke
to the hag, "Where are we?"

The old woman's head jerked,
startled, as if she didn't realize there
was another prisoner. "What?"
she said in a hoarse grumble.

"Where is this place?"

"The new ones always want
to know where they are and
who's got them." She chuckled,
as much to herself as to the new
prisoner. "Who cares, is what
I say. Once she's got you, you'll
never get free. No one has."

"I know that Aneurin means
to enslave us, and this dungeon
is somewhere within her village. But, where in her village.
Can you tell me, old woman?"

"Old woman? Don't ever call
me that. I am Silat, daughter of
the herdsman, Thun, and his wife
Tilda, my mother. My home is in
Garsin, but I'll never see it again.
And you'll never see yours neither!"

"Damn it, woman. Answer
my question!"

"You don't scare me. You're
as powerless as I, even with your
brawn and bragging mouth. They
won't last in this place. You'll
never leave, mark my words."

"You're a fool if you think this
sorceress can hold me forever. Now
tell me where she has the children."

"Oh, the children. That's the vile
diablerie of this place. The inno-
cents; slaves they are, with minds
too callow to defend themselves
against her spells. Old enough to
work, yes, I should say so, but too
meek to fend off her magik."

"Where does she keep them?"

"Oh, don't you worry about

that. Culleen rounds them up and sets them to work. Keeps 'em busy from first meal to last. She's a tetchy one, too."

"Who is this Culleen?"

"I told you, she runs everything for the mistress. Maybe they're sisters. Must be, otherwise why would she help her like that? Sister Culleen, that's who she is."

It seemed useless to talk to the hag. The time passed slowly in silence. Kragar could not break free, but he strained at his bonds all the same, testing them, determined to escape. He questioned Silat from time to time, but her responses reflected her fractured view. With no hope of escape, she'd stopped looking for an edge or anything that might be useful about the village or her captor.

As the faint light that filtered into the dungeon faded, Kragar heard the scuffling of feet and saw the glow of candlelight approach. A young woman appeared with two small buckets suspended by their handles on her forearm. Her ashen face was dower, her eyes lowered in submission. Strands of brown hair hung down from the scarf wrapped around her head. She set the buckets on the stone floor to free her arm. It looked as if the burden of enslavement had added a few years to her young life. Kragar strained for a better look at her face, but the candlelight was behind her, and she kept her head bowed low.

The smell of stew or broth reached his nose, and Kragar realized at once how hungry he was. The woman served Silat first, fixing the bucket handle around the captive's neck so the bucket lay against her chest beneath her

chin. The woman gently brushed Silat's hair away from her face and inserted a thick tube into the soup.

"Your meat and vegetables are finely chopped. You should have no problem sucking them through the cylinder."

"Are you Culleen?" asked Kragar as the woman bent for his bucket.

She nodded and reached up on her toes to fasten the vessel around his neck.

"Where are the children?" he asked. "Where do they sleep?"

"No," said Culleen. "I'm not to talk to prisoners."

"Oh, save your groveling for when the mistress is around to appreciate it," said Silat. "Tell him what he wants to know. He seems stupid, but perhaps he'll catch on in time."

Culleen nodded, her eyes wide as she stared at Silat. "Yes, ma'am" she said. She turned her face back toward Kragar, placed a metal tube in his broth, and stepped back. "The children sleep in the hall of residence, below centerhouse. That's enough now. Drink your soup, you're only allowed a few minutes."

The soup was thin with a few slivered chunks. Kragar continued questioning the woman between gulps. "How are the children made to serve your mistress?"

Culleen rocked gently back and forth on the stone floor, her arms wrapped around her knees. "We all serve the mistress," she said. "A privilege and our only pleasure."

"Has anyone ever escaped?"

Silat cackled. "You are a foolish dolt, aren't you? Well nevermind, fools never learn."

"Mind your tongue woman," said Kragar. "When I arrived here I carried with me a broadsword and a skinning dagger. Where can I find them?"

Culleen reached up and removed the bucket from Kragar's neck in silence. Then she turned to Silat. "Are you finished, ma'am?" she asked.

"Yes, it was delicious."

Culleen nodded, gathered the buckets and candle and shuffled out of sight leaving the prisoners in darkness.

The impenetrable black seemed to absorb all sound as well as light. Kragar could hear nothing of his fellow prisoner, no moan spurred from aching muscles, no rustle of motion, not even the puff of her foul breath. That suited him sufficiently. He'd gathered as much information as he needed. He wondered why she was strung up with him. Perhaps she was posted there to keep him under watchful eyes.

He turned his attention to his bonds. His muscles bulged as he pulled against the heavy straps. He tested their strength from different directions, until he found the one that gave him the greatest leverage, pushing his back and heels against the wall. But the effort was useless. The straps were thick and carefully crafted. He could not snap them and there was nothing of any use to wear them away. He could not escape his bonds. The strain of his captivity had taken its toll. He recalled Zeya's warning, ". . . she deadens their wills with potions." He knew in the morning he must make his stand, but hadn't yet formed a solid plan of battle. He relaxed his troubled mind and soon fell asleep despite of the discomfort of hanging from his arms.

He woke to the sound of a gravelly voice. "It's time I put you to work, barbarian."

Before him floated the sorceress, bathed in the light of two torches fastened to the opposite wall. She was cloaked in a black burnoose that covered her entirely save her wrinkled, ashen face. She held Kragar's skinning dagger and tipped his head erect with the end of its blade.

"I would sooner die than serve as your slave," Kragar said through his teeth.

"We shall see," said Aneurin. "But first, the morning meal."

Culleen appeared from the shadows with buckets of food for the prisoners. She arranged them as the night before and waited for the prisoners to finish.

Although he hungered, Kragar only pretended to drink. His thoughts turned to Silat. Why was she here? What purpose did she serve bound as he, wasting away in the dungeon? She should be toiling with the children, spellbound by

Aneurin. Suddenly, he knew! The name "Silat" when reversed, spelt "Talis", the talisman of the sorceress. He bellowed the forbidden name.

Aneurin shuttered and choked at the sound of her secret exposed, fading into the netherworld from which she had come. The dagger she'd held clattered to the stone floor. Kragar turned. Silat's bonds had dissolved. The bucket around her neck fell, spilling its contents on the dungeon floor. The sorceress was no longer old. Her wrinkled face was now smooth and youthful, her ragged clothing no longer cloaking her colorful silks. She darted toward the knife, but Culleen too was no longer spellbound. The caregiver thrust Silat aside and scooped up the blade. Rather than risk an uneven fight, the sorceress turned and ran from the dungeon. Culleen quickly cut Kragar's bonds. He unhooked the bucket from his neck, snatched the weapon from the caregiver, and raced after Silat, shouting her talisman again, to subvert her powers.

Scrambling up a flight of stairs, Kragar emerged in the light of day. At first the daylight was blinding, but he could see Silat before him, standing her ground, wielding his broadsword. She rushed forward, swinging the great blade. Kragar rolled to avoid her thrust, then sprung to his feet to face her anew.

She came again. He parried her blow just enough to deflect it, but they could both see his dagger was no match for the broadsword. A smile curled the corners of Silat's mouth as she lunged forward. Again Kragar dodged her strike, this time rolling twice to put distance between them. When he came up, he hurled the dagger, as she rushed toward him. His aim was true, but the dagger merely bounced off her chest, tumbling to the ground. Impossible, unless she wore a coat of mail beneath her silks.

He barely evaded her blade, ducking under her swing, slamming his arm against her back as he scrambled past. The force threw her to the ground as he plunged deeper into the village, frantically scanning the grounds for a suitable weapon. He did not glance backward, but could hear her pursuit behind him. He was much fasted than his foe, but he knew he must remain in her presence or risk the return of her sorcery.

Her anger fueled her chase for a moment, but as Kragar drew her toward a stack of logs, she suddenly stopped and turned away. Kragar raced forward, his eyes scanning the worksite. He spotted a double-bladed axe and grabbed its stout handle—and froze.

Silat had finally realized her folly and backed away from him. Once she was out of his sight, her powers returned and she cast a paralyzing spell upon him. Now, she sauntered toward him at her leisure, carving up the air in lazy arcs with the broadsword as she approached.

Kragar stood helplessly rigidly upright, arms at his sides, as she advanced. His right hand still grasped the axe, but no matter how much his mind struggled to break the paralysis, he could not. Now, Silat stood before him, in battle stance. She drew the broadsword back, grasping its hilt in both hands, ready to strike.

"Talis!" Culleen's voice cut through the silence from behind the sorceress.

Kragar lurched back as he

desire; to return to their homes. Kragar and Culleen helped them gather the supplies and blankets they would require for the journey.

Three days later, a caravan of children, led by Kragar, with Culleen posted at the rear, broached the outskirts of Aldwier. Word traveled as if lightning, and soon the entire village poured out of its fields, stables, and houses to join the procession as it made its way to the towncenter. The council of elders, Perth, the parents of the abductees, and their children wept with joy at the reunion.

Kragar presented Silat's necklace to Perth. The warrior and Culleen regaled the elders and the villagers with the story of their children's rescue. A tale told again and again long into the night as the village celebrated and drank to the warrior's health until slumber finally claimed them.

The following morning, Perth and Culleen gathered the children taken from surrounding villages. Loading them into a covered wagon, the priest and caregiver set off for all the places from which the children had come.

Kragar bid farewell to his new friends and set out upon the road toward new adventures. But that would be later. He'd split his bounty with Culleen, for he may well not have succeeded without her aid. The 24 golds packed safely in his saddlebags would last a good long while. He was ready to enjoy the spoils of victory—plenty of mead, fresh meat, and the company of a willing woman in the next township he encountered along the road.

swung his axe straight up. His reach was longer than he foe's, so while her swing cleaved the air a mere inch from his neck, his shattered her jaw with the axe, driving her head back so hard it snapped her neck. She was dead before her body tumbled to the ground.

Kragar knelt to retrieve his sword and wrenched the necklace around Silat's throat free—proof enough the sorceress would trouble him nor the village Aldwier again.

As he stood, Culleen rushed forward and embraced him, each thankful to the other. The caregiver's face overflowing with joy. A moment later, from all around, they could hear the sound of children's voices growing nearer. Free will had returned to all.

Culleen gathered the laughing, crying, chattering youth as Kragar carried Silat's body into the dungeon and sealed its entrance with stones.

Now clear-eyed and exuberant, the children all shared a single

THE BEAUTIFUL CIGAR GIRL

or She loved not wisely, but too widely

by LEO MARR

Leo Marr that appeared in *Mystery Book Magazine* while it was still a digest; this is, after all, *The Digest Enthusiast*, so the pulp issues of the magazine will have to wait.

Mystery Book Magazine No. 2 August 1945
The Beautiful Cigar Girl (or, She loved not wisely, but too widely)

The first true-crime article concerns the 1841 murder of Mary Cecilia Rogers in New York. Marr writes that Edgar Allan Poe based his story, "The Mystery of Marie Roget," on this sensational news item. The real murder, if it was a murder, was never solved. There was suspicion that the young woman's death was caused by a botched abortion and that it was made to look like murder in order to conceal the truth.

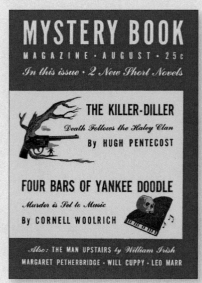

**Mystery Book Magazine No. 4
October 1945**
Barnum Had a Baby
(or, The Horrid Fate of the
Amorous Dentist)

Another murder in New York is examined, this time, the 1857 killing of dentist Harvey Burdell. "He was the possessor of a rare talent, amounting almost to genius. He could alienate friends and influence people—to wreak bodily harm on him." This is another unsolved murder with too many suspects. The title comes from a display by P.T. Barnum in his Broadway Museum; that fact has a tangential relationship to the murder, but it played on what was a sensational story at the time.

THE WOMAN WAS FRAIL

Or a Mistress in Her own House

by LEO MARR

**Mystery Book Magazine No. 5
November 1945**

The Woman was Frail
(or, a Mistress in Her own House)

William and Lucretia Chapman
run a school in Andalusia, Pennsylvania, in 1831, and are visited
by Don Lino Amalia Esposimina,
who claims to be the son of the
governor of California. He spins
a tale of woe and Lucretia agrees
to let him stay with them for three
years while he pays her to teach
him proper English. The relationship between teacher and student
becomes romantic and, before you
know it, William Chapman grows
violently ill and dies, soon to be
replaced as Lucretia's husband by
Don Lino. After the Don steals all he
can from his new bride, he departs,
and she suddenly realizes that he
was a scoundrel and a poisoner.
Arrested in New England, Don Lino
is brought to Philadelphia to stand
trial for the murder, along with
Lucretia. Though she is acquitted
and he is convicted, the governor
later grants him a full pardon!

DEATH OF THE HOUSEKEEPER'S COUSIN

or, who made Elma's sands run out?

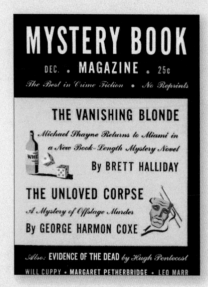

Mystery Book Magazine No. 6 December 1945

Death of the Housekeeper's Cousin (or, who made Elma's sands run out?)

Said to be New York's "first full-fledged murder mystery," the December 1799 disappearance of Elma Sands on the eve of her wedding is followed by the discovery of her body at the bottom of a well ten days later on property owned by Aaron Burr. Her betrothed, Levi Weeks, is put on trial for her murder and two of his lawyers are Burr and Alexander Hamilton. The prosecution's case is destroyed by skilled cross-examination of witnesses and Weeks is acquitted, but he later flees the city in disgrace and the murder is never solved.

by LEO MARR

Mystery Book Magazine No. 7 January 1946

Death in the Double Standard (or, the Sad Fate of Mrs. Dan Sickles' Lover)

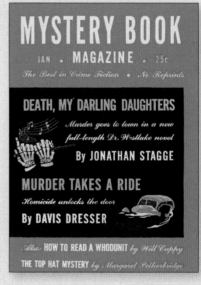

Life isn't all roses for New York Congressman Dan Sickles in 1859; married to a woman 16 years his junior, he begins to suspect that she is having a torrid affair with U.S. District Attorney Philip Barton Key (son of Francis Scott Key). His worst fears are realized when an anonymous letter provides details of the couple's trysting place. After forcing a confession out of his bride, Sickles shoots and kills his rival and stands trial for murder. The proceedings focus on his late wife's infidelity and he is acquitted, but the notoriety he gains thwarts his presidential aspirations. He later becomes a war hero at Gettysburg (this is disputed by historians today), becomes Minister to Spain, and lover of Queen Isabella, living to the ripe old age of 94!

A CADAVER A DAY

or, Ghouls

of Old

Edinburgh

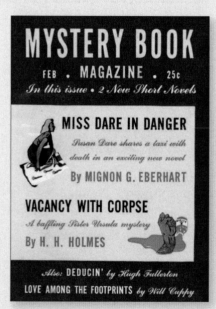

**Mystery Book Magazine No. 8
February 1946**
A Cadaver a Day
(or, Ghouls of Old Edinburgh)

 The oft-told tale of Burke and Hare is examined; the two Resurrectionists supply bodies in Edinburgh in the late 1820s to Dr. Knox at the local medical school, creating their own corpses when the graveyard cannot keep up with the demand. On Halloween Night 1828, party guests discover a body and the police are called. Hare turns on Burke and assists the cops; though there were sixteen murders in all, only three formal charges are brought. Burke is convicted and, before a crowd of 25,000, he is given the same fate as his victims: suffocation followed by dissection. Hare flees the country and disappears, while Dr. Knox's career goes steadily downhill and he ends up a lecturer for a traveling medicine show!

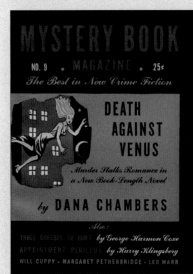

**Mystery Book Magazine No. 9
March 1946**

Death of the Vanishing Chin
(or, Dr. Parkman collects more
than his due)

Dr. George Parkman of Boston is known as "The Chin" due to his immense, protruding jaw. He disappears on November 23, 1849, at Harvard Medical College and chemistry professor John Webster is arrested for his murder after parts of Parkman's dismembered body are found by a janitor. He is tried in March 1850, found guilty, and later confesses; he is hanged in August of that year.

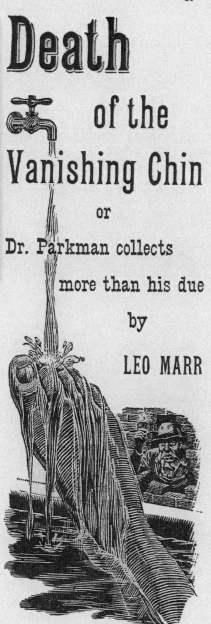

Death
of the
Vanishing Chin
or
Dr. Parkman collects
more than his due
by
LEO MARR

Death in the house on 23rd. street

Mystery Book Magazine No. 10 April 1946

Death in the house on 23rd street (or, a Philanthropist's Untimely End)

Prominent New York philanthropist Benjamin Nathan is robbed and beaten to death in his home on July 29, 1870. A bloody handprint is found on the wall, but this is before the science of fingerprints came into being and so the murder remains unsolved.

the Ghost went west

Or, Confession is Bad for the Soul

By LEO MARR

Mystery Book Magazine No. 11 May 1946

The Ghost Went West
(or, Confession is Bad for the Soul)

Living in Vermont in the year 1812, did Stephen Boorn kill his sister's husband, Russell Colvin, in a fight, or did Colvin flee over the Green Mountains, as he had done so many times before? Boorn later writes out a confession and is sentenced to death, but his conviction is vacated when Colvin turns up, hale and hearty!

by
LEO
MARR

Mystery Book Magazine No. 13 August 1946
The Parson Passes
(or, who hanged Sarah Maria Cornell?)

The December 1832 murder of Sarah Cornell in Rhode Island led to "the first trial of a clergyman for the crime of murder in these United States." Her body was found in a haystack, hanging from a rope around her neck. Based on a letter found among her possessions, Reverend Mr. Avery was arrested for murder and his alibi is flimsy: he claims to have been out for a solitary walk when she was killed. Avery had banished the woman from his Methodist church due to her ill repute, and she was found to have been with child when she died. Though the charges did not stick and Avery was released, a public outcry forced him to leave the area; he was eventually tracked down by a man named Harvey Harnden, who wrote a pamphlet about a search that Marr calls "the first detective story." Avery stood trial but was acquitted and the killer was never identified.

by *Leo Marr*

The DEPILATORY DUKE

A DETECTIVE WHO DIDN'T SPLIT HAIRS

Mystery Book Magazine No. 15 October 1946

The Depilatory Duke
(A Detective Who Didn't Split Hairs)

Inspector Pierre Allard of the Surete investigates the murder of Fanny, Duchess de Praslin, in 1848 Paris, and Marr suggests that he was likely a prototype for Sherlock Holmes. The Duchess's husband, the Duke, is having an affair with the family governess and, while Allard suspects him of the crime, he knows that making an accusation would be dangerous. Yet arrest the Duke he does, setting the city on edge in that revolutionary year. In an early example of the scientific method of detection, hairs stuck to the murder weapon serve as proof, and the Duke conveniently commits suicide in his jail cell.

led to a Staten Island dentist named Kennedy, who is arrested and tried for murder in 1899. Despite an alibi and uncertain witnesses, he is found guilty and sentenced to death, but new evidence leads to a second trial and then a third, both of which end in a hung jury. Dr. Kennedy is released, and the case is never solved.

Mystery Book Magazine No. 16 November 1946

The Beautiful Body in Suite 84
(or, Horses Shouldn't Bet on People)

In New York City again, this time at the Grand Hotel at Broadway and 31st Street in the year 1898, a maid finds the dead body of a beautiful young woman who was killed by a blow from a lead pipe to her head. She had registered the day before as Mrs. Maxwell of Brooklyn, but investigation reveals her real name to be Dolly Reynolds. Her husband is a stockbroker by the name of Maurice Mendham, but another maid identifies him as a Mr. Reynolds who shared a house with Dolly on 58th Street. Further clues

IF YOU KNEW SUSI

by LEO MARR

Mystery Book Magazine No. 17
January 1947
If You Knew Susi
(or, Arsenic and Old Fly-Paper)

In 1840s Hungary, midwife Susi Olah has a busy practice among farmers who cannot afford more children. Nine women die at her hands, yet nine trials end in her exoneration. Eventually, she poisons all of the other midwives in the area, thus eliminating any competition. She begins to sell arsenic to wives to feed to their abusive spouses; she even poisons her own husband and son—her husband dies, but her son survives and flees the area. Soon, Susi becomes a central figure in the local battle of the sexes that rages for twenty years. At last, she is tried and convicted of the murder of a woman's 70-year-old mother; this is followed by the arrest of dozens of women, all of whom are hauled into court. When the situation begins to look impossible for Susi, she solves the problem by hanging herself.

MAGAZINE • NO. 17 • 25c

A NEW COMPLETE NOVEL

THE SILVER LEOPARD

Rich Man, Artist, Laborer, Thief — Are Victims in Inspector McKee's Latest Case

by HELEN REILLY

ALSO: Death Comes to the Carnival in A VOICE BEHIND HIM by FREDRIC BROWN

the Farmer takes a life

by
LEO
MARR

or Belle was such
a cut-up

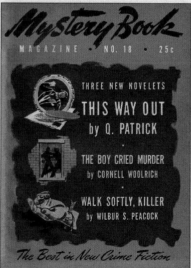

Mystery Book Magazine No. 18 March 1947

The Farmer Takes a Life
(or, Belle was such a cut-up)

Near the turn of the (twentieth) century, the Gunness farmhouse burns down one April and the corpses of three Gunness children and a headless woman are discovered in the ashes. Belle Gunness was a strong, stout widow who had bought the farm and married Pete Gunness, who died seven months later when a sausage grinder fell on his head. As a widow with three children and a farm, she had many suitors, two of whom arrived with cash in hand and quickly disappeared. When suspicion began to arise, the house burned down, but was the headless corpse Belle's? The body is nowhere near as stout as she had been in life and, when the sheriff's party begins to dig around the house, they find pieces of over 100 bodies. A farmhand claims that Belle killed her prospective husbands with an axe and chopped them up in the cellar. It is thought that she killed another woman and beheaded her to make identification impossible before setting off with her money.

Above: Supporting illustration for Leo Marr's "The Morals of Marquise Marie" from issue 19. The cover of issue 19 is shown on the back cover of this issue of *The Digest Enthusiast*.

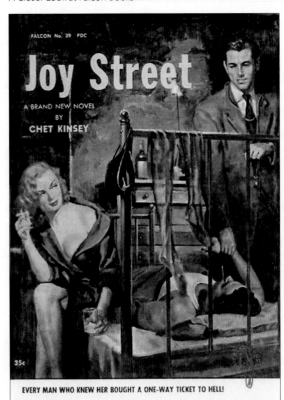

Falcon Books were published by the same outfit that published similar sexy digest series, Exotic Books, Ecstasy Books, and Rainbow Books, but none of those had the accent on mystery and crime that the Falcons did.

Falcon Books

- ☐ 21 *Season for Sin* by Anthony Scott (Brett Halliday)
- ☐ 22 *The Scarlet Bride* by Mark Reed (Norman A. Daniels)
- ☐ 23 *Mabel and Men!* by George Bottari
- ☐ 24 *Three for Passion* by Hodge Evens (Dudley Dean McGaughy)
- ☐ 25 *The Case of the Cancelled Redhead* by Hamlin Daly (E. Hoffman Price)
- ☐ 26 *Lay Down and Die!* by Mark Reed (Norman A. Daniels)
- ☐ 27 *Lida Lynn* by Norma Dann (Norman A. Daniels)
- ☐ 28 *Girls Out of Hell* by Joe Weiss
- ☐ 29 *Mistress on a Deathbed!* by Norman A. Daniels
- ☐ 30 *Daggar of Flesh* by Richard A. Prather
- ☐ 31 *Slave Girl* by Tom Roan
- ☐ 32 *Sins of the Flesh* by Mark Reed (Norman A. Daniels)
- ☐ 33 *Yellow-Head!* by Hodge Evens (Dudley Dean McGaughy)
- ☐ 34 *Shack Girl!* by Norma Dann (Norman A. Daniels)
- ☐ 35 *Raise the Devil!* by David Wade (Norman A. Daniels)
- ☐ 36 *Junkie* by Jonathan Craig
- ☐ 37 *Woman Hunter* by Laura Hale (Fredric Lorenz)
- ☐ 38 *Sweet Savage* by Norman A. Daniels
- ☐ 39 *Joy Street* by Chet Kinsey
- ☐ 40 *Whip-Hand!* by Hodge Evens (Dudley Dean McGaughy)
- ☐ 41 *The Evil Sleep* by Evan Hunter
- ☐ 42 *The Long Night* by Bryce Walton
- ☐ 43 *House of 1,000 Desires* by Mark Reed (Norman A. Daniels)
- ☐ 44 *Honky Tonk Girl* by Charles Beckman, Jr.

DIGEST F&SF CLASSICS

Article by Steve Carper

"But during 1918 and 1919 three major names emerged who would lead SF on into the next stage of its evolution: Abraham Merritt, Murray Leinster and Ray Cummings. Merritt, certainly to be numbered among the greatest of all fantasy writers, was the harbinger."

–*Science Fiction, Fantasy, and Weird Fiction Magazines* by Marshall B. Tymn and Mike Ashley pgs 105–106 Greenwood Press 1985

Avon Murder of the Month/ Murder Mystery Monthly

In 1939, Robert DeGraff unhinged the American publishing world by introducing Pocket Books. Though he was clearly imitating the English paperback Penguin Books, which started by ripping-off the German Albatross/Tauchnitz Books, American publishers were certain that Americans didn't want mass-market sized paperbacks and publishers couldn't possibly make a profit on them. Boy, were they ever wrong. Although the first set of ten Pocket Books had a limited distribution of 10,000 copies only in New York City, they almost instantly became a national

sensation and started selling in the millions. The term pocketbooks became a generic and so did the 25¢ price, so familiar and so standard that it didn't need to be printed on the books themselves for Pocket or any of its numerous imitators.

Pocket Books gained national distribution through the giant American News Company (ANC), which had 400 U.S. branches servicing tens of thousands of newsstands, drug stores, discount stores and other venues, making the books available everywhere. They were too successful. Pocket Books grew so big that in 1941 it broke from ANC to contract with independent distributors, soon reaching 100,000

Interior art from *Murder of the Month* No. 1, 1942. Opposite: page 8. Above: page 69.

outlets. ANC told Joseph Meyers, the publisher of one of its subsidiaries, the J. S. Ogilvie Publishing Company (mentioned as the earliest publisher of digest-sized Photoplay Editions in my article of that name in *TDE* No. 12, June 2020), to start a mass-market division of ANC's own. Ogilvie became Avon Pocket-Sized Books and released its first dozen titles on November 1, 1941.

Half of those books were mysteries, the genre that absolutely dominated mass-market publishing in the 1940s. A dedicated mystery line made loads of sense. The Mercury Press already had two in digest size, Mercury and Bestseller. What Mercury didn't have was a mass-market line. Why Avon immediately started a digest-sized mystery line to compete with its mass-market titles is itself a mystery. The larger format must have been far more expensive to print and probably would have sold less, since mass-market paperbacks could be placed on convenient rotating racks anywhere, whereas digest-sized books normally sold only alongside magazines.

Nevertheless, January 1942 saw the release of the unnumbered first title in the Murder of the Month line, A. Merritt's *Seven Footprints to Satan*. Under the heading "Good News for Mystery Fans," the inside front cover explained the rationale of the endeavor.

Murder of the Month No. 1, 1942
Seven Footprints to Satan by A. Merritt.

Murder Mystery Monthly No. 5, 1942 *Burn Witch Burn* by A. Merritt. Cover by William Forrest.

MURDER OF THE MONTH titles are printed on good paper with bold, clear type and strongly bound with a decorative cover in full color, finished off with a hard, glossy surface. A further innovation are the unusual illustrations throughout each volume by world-famous artists, to add to your enjoyment whilst reading the story.

You'd think a "world-famous" (though never named) artist would charge a bundle for providing the fifteen illustrations scattered through the 310 numbered pages. Yes, 310 pages, a book "complete and unexpurgated." Those familiar with digest novels know that even after wartime paper restrictions were lifted, the vast majority of them were abridged to fit into 128 pages on thin paper bulking no more than ¼ inch thick. *Satan* is as hefty as a hardcover, more than ¾ inch in depth, and vastly less convenient than the literal pocket-sized mass-

market paperbacks. Perhaps the expectation was to give buyers the psychological feeling of getting more for their 25¢. Whatever the reasoning, the war forced Avon books to rapidly slim down, the illustrations vanishing along with the bulk.

Just as mysterious a mystery is the name of the author picked to launch this high-end new mystery series.

"An extremely strong list of authors has been arranged for MURDER OF THE MONTH, among which are included: A. Merritt, editor of the American Weekly, who is a past-master in the art of mystery writing…" [italics omitted as in original]

Abraham Grace Merritt is almost forgotten today, so it's startling to go back through the records and find he was one of the most famous writers in America for more than a decade. Just a few years earlier, in 1938, *Argosy*, the premier pulp

Murder Mystery Monthly No. 11, 1943 *Creep, Shadow, Creep* by A. Merritt. Cover by William Forrest.

Murder Mystery Monthly No. 18, 1944 *The Moon Pool* by A. Merritt.

fiction magazine (whose many variant names I'm ignoring), held a contest to reprint the most popular story from its 58 years of publication. Readers had a lot to choose from: the magazine's pages spawned more than 700 hardcovers, many of them world famous. Merritt's *The Ship of Ishtar* won.

Merritt is that rarest of specimens, an author who didn't start writing until he was already well-to-do. He was appointed assistant editor of *The American Weekly* magazine in 1912 at the age of 26. By 1919, his salary hit $25,000. After he took over as editor in 1937 he made $100,000. As a sideline, he published his first story in 1917, for *Argosy* of course. Eight novels followed, marking him as the foremost American author of fantasy of his age. His popularity began to diminish after his unexpected death in 1943 but he has the honor of being the first F&SF writer to have a magazine

with his name in the title, the short-lived (and non-digest) *A. Merritt's Fantasy Magazine* from 1949–1950.

Fantasy is not mystery. Merritt couldn't write an intellectual whodunit or a gritty hardboiled tale with an enchanted dagger pointed at his head. *Satan* is the closest to the genre he ever got, more Sax Rohmer than Arthur Conan Doyle. A contemporary reviewer wrote, "Here is a fantastic tale, thrilling in every page, and a plot that could not possibly happen in seven hundred years. That is one reason it is extra good reading—it is all so impossible." That's Merritt in a nutshell.

Satan first appeared as a five-part serial in *Argosy* in 1927 and was published in hardcovers in February 1928. It went through three editions the first month, had a low-price reprint hardback edition, and was made into a film released in January 1929. Sam Moskowitz, in a 1959 article, claimed that

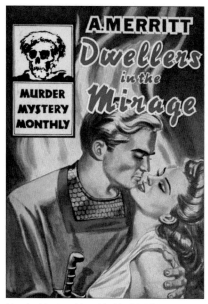

Murder Mystery Monthly No. 24, 1944
Dwellers in the Mirage by A. Merritt.

Murder Mystery Monthly No. 29, 1945 *The Face
in the Abyss* by A. Merritt. Cover by Paul Stahr.

the book sold a million copies for Avon, presumably including those from the mass-market editions in 1943 (unnumbered but No. 26 in release), 1950 (Avon No. 235), 1955 (Avon T-115), and 1957 (Avon T-208). Avon never listed printings, but it's known that some titles were reprinted more than once.

Avon released all seven other Merritt novels (though one is a fix-up of two novelettes) in digest format when the line was retitled Murder Mystery Monthly. (Every other Avon digest line has Avon as part of the title, from *Avon Annual* to *Avon Western Reader*. Only this imprint is not credited to Avon on the cover, although the name is prominent inside.) All seven, along with a short-story collection *The Fox Woman* (Avon 214, 1959), were released in mass-market format under eleven numbers by the time of Moskowitz's article. He quoted

Avon as saying that they had sold upward of 4,000,000 copies in total. Merritt was a superstar.

Bonded Special

Leslie Charteris, the author of The Saint mysteries, was another superstar of the pulp era whose fame has diminished over the years. In 1945, immediately after the war's end (copyright registrations begin in September) when paper restrictions were lifted, he joined with Anson Bond to launch a digest-sized series of books under Bond's name, one of the extremely rare Los Angeles paperback publishing trials. Six Saint novels or collections plus four *The Saint's Choice* of anthologies—*English Crime, American Crime, True Crime Stories,* and *Humorous Crime Stories*—started the line. (To confuse bibliographers, the first novel, *Lady on a Train,* a Photoplay Edition, had no number, and then

Murder Mystery Monthly No. 34, 1945
The Ship of Ishtar by A. Merritt. Cover by
Paul Stahr.

Murder Mystery Monthly No. 41, 1946
The Metal Monster by A. Merritt. Cover by
Paul Stahr.

numbers one through nine followed.) Graham Holroyd, in his *Paperback Price Guide*, calls them Bonded Books, and both Kevin Hancer and Kenneth R. Johnson lists them merely as Bonded. But each of them is labeled A BONDED MYSTERY in large letters across the front cover. That stayed true for numbers ten through sixteen, which offered books by other West Coast writers like Paul Cain and Craig Rice. All were, naturally, mysteries.

But what about other genres? They were a problem. Up through 1945, paperbacks in general and digests to an even greater extent were so completely identified with mysteries that little room remained for interlopers. Bond apparently wanted to try an experiment. He inserted two books into the middle of his crime lineup. You might ask how, given that all the numbers from one

to sixteen were already in use. Simple. They were labeled 10A and 10B.

Oscar J. Friend was an old-time pulpster who wrote in many genres under many names. Like Cain and Rice, he also put in a stint as a Hollywood screenwriter. He became a force in science fiction as an agent for many of the top writers and also worked as the wartime editor for a couple of magazines. However, his book, 10B, was a Bonded Western, *Guns of Powder River*.

It was 10A that was science fiction, although the term had such low standing in 1945 that the cover actually called it a Bonded Special. Nothing could have been more timely than to publish a Malcolm Jameson story titled *Atomic Bomb* in late 1945. Or less honest. No atomic bomb or atomic war appears in this silly misuse of science. The accurate depiction is given by the

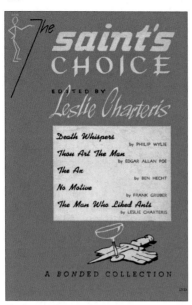

The Saint's Choice Volume 2, 1945.

Bonded Special No. 10A, 1945
Atomic Bomb by Malcolm James.

story's original December 1943 title, "The Giant Atom." That's a literal rather than figurative description. In a scenario that would play out in dozens of Hollywood movies in the 1950s, the stalwart hero fights an implacable monster, in this case a giant-size single atom that absorbs everything in sight. The blurb in the original magazine appearance was:

> "Only Steve Bennion, Inventive Genius, and His Lovely Assistant, Kitty Pennell, Stand Between the Earth and Destruction When a Flaming Monster Threatens to Devour and Destroy Civilization"

The editor that accepted this horror novel written with a vocabulary set of physics refrigerator magnets? Oscar J. Friend. I have to assume that he suggested the repurposing of the story to take advantage of recent headlines because Jameson, not a West Coaster, had in April died of cancer and couldn't complain.

Taller and slimmer than the Bonded Mysteries at 7.5 x 5 inches, 10A and 10B were stapled rather than perfect-bound and with much flimsier covers. Trying to find one today in decent shape will consume your time and money. They may have been meant to survey the market for western and science fiction lines in the cheapest possible fashion.

Numerous western digest lines did appear starting in 1947 and the Galaxy Science Fiction Novel line started in 1950, but Charteris and Bond had a falling-out in 1946. Charteris continued the Bonded numbering under the Chartered imprint. Bond immediately started his own line, called, to later consternation, Bonded Mysteries. Their covers can be distinguished by the use of a red seal containing the words. Only the first four were digests. None of the titles were by Charteris, of course, but Bond continued his

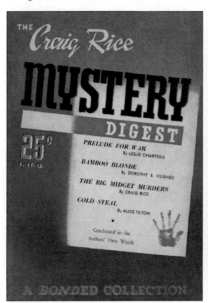

The Craig Rice Mystery Digest No. 1, 1945.

Century Adventure No. 104, 1947
The Green Man by Harold M. Sherman.

association with Rice and so is of interest to digest historians. He followed up Bonded 12, the *Craig Rice Mystery Digest*, with two 1945 issues of the *Craig Rice Crime Digest* magazine. When that failed, he tried again in 1946 with the digest-sized *Movie Mystery Magazine*, which contained a movie novelization in each of the three issues, one of them being a movie made from a Rice novel, *Home Sweet Homicide.*

Century

This was another ANC imprint, headquartered in Chicago. Rather than be tied to one type of novel, Century did a mix of everything, some labeled—Century Mystery, Century Western—some not. Unusually, it featured many romance novels and even some "Southern" novels. You never knew what would be on the newsstand next: Century did its first 64 books in digest format but then started

intermixing them with mass-market-sized titles through No. 99. Books No. 105–136 were all mass-market. For some reason, No. 100–104 were again digest sized.

Once again, though, science fiction didn't qualify as a genre. Century's last digest, No. 104, was true science fiction, reprinted from the pages of the October 1946 *Amazing Stories.* Nevertheless it got labeled the same as Century No. 100–103, as a Century Adventure. (Merit, an offshoot of Century, would publish two books labeled as science fiction, but that wouldn't be until the far future of 1950 and 1951, showing what an enormous change in public perception five years made.) Harold Morrow Sherman wasn't known for F&SF: virtually all his dozens of earlier short stories stretching back to the mid-1920s appeared in *Boy's Life.* *The Green Man* was his first venture into science fiction, followed by three more stories for editor Ray

Handi-Books No. 62, 1947 *The Murder of the U.S.A.* by Will F. Jenkins.

Palmer. That probably wasn't coincidental. One of Sherman's dozen or so series of boy's novels featured adventures to lost worlds and his latest book detailed his experiments in telepathy, both subjects that Palmer loved palming off on his readers.

The Green Man is a first-contact satire about a green visitor from a planet "a trillion miles away" who gets caught up in the frenzied popular culture hype Sherman knew from working in Hollywood. Sherman wrote a sequel, "The Green Man Returns," that appeared in the December 1947 *Amazing*. Neither appeared in any other format until 21st century publishers started resurrecting almost every scrap from Golden Age SF. Even so, the double-dose of green makes one wonder if this were an impetus for the little green men from outer space trope.

The publication date of Century No. 104 is not certain. Holroyd lists

it as 1946, but after earlier numbers listed as 1947. The ISFDB.com also has it as 1946. That would imply a quick turnaround for a story that probably hit newsstands in September of that year, but a possible one. The fact that a large number of Century Books with lower numbers bear 1947 dates and no other titles with 1946 dates are known to follow them makes me side with a 1947 printing.

Handi-Books

James L. Quinn's name bobs up occasionally in digest publishing, although nothing about him other than the name seems to be known. He apparently had some connection to the book business when he started Handi-Books in New York in 1941. The company's address moves upstate to Kingston in 1945 and, perhaps not coincidentally, Handi-Books stopped being stapled and became perfect bound. That line stopped in 1951. In 1952 the Quinn Publishing Company was now in Buffalo and started two digests, *If*, Worlds of Science Fiction, and *Strange*, The Magazine of True Mystery, which lasted only three issues. Quinn even became editor of *If* for a few years. All that can be said is that he must have had a day job.

Mercury Mystery was the first modern digest-sized line, launched in 1937. In 1939 Pocket Books started American mass-market publishing. So revolutionary were they that they had no real competition until 1941, when both Avon and Handi-Books started. The name Handi-Books was meant to invoke convenience, the way Pocket Books' name instantly told you where the book would fit. At 6¼ x 4½ inches (dimensions changed slightly over time) they were barely larger than a mass-market book and cheaper as well, a mere 15¢ at first. They would fit in a man's suit pocket or a woman's purse.

Handi-Books published only mysteries until 1947, so they also faced the question of how to fit in a science fiction yarn. By calling it a mystery, of course. Murray Leinster had been publishing science fiction for almost 30 years in 1946, but under his real name of Will F. Jenkins he published across a range of genres. In 1946, mainstream publisher Crown put out what may be the first of the post-WWII atomic war novels, titled *The Murder of the U.S.A.*, marketed as a mystery. The mystery is what country destroyed the U.S. with an atomic missile barrage and how to use science to prevent further damage. Jenkins forecast underground missile bunkers with hidden nukes for retaliation, as prescient as his almost uncannily-accurate depiction of the internet in his Murray Leinster short story "A Logic Named Joe," also from 1946. Mainstream mystery reviewers called it "a little gem" and "far better than the general run of 'science fiction.'"

Magabook

Editor Horace Gold splashed into the sleepy, shallow pool of science fiction with big ideas of changing the field forever. In late 1950 he started both the *Galaxy Science Fiction* magazine and the Galaxy Science Fiction Novels line, avowing to print new, modern, and bold works that would supersede the whiff of mustiness from John W. Campbell's *Astounding Science Fiction* and whatever the hell Ray Palmer was doing

Magabook No. 1, 1963 *The Sky Is Falling/ Badge of Infamy* by Lester del Rey. Cover by Virgil Finlay.

at *Amazing Stories*. The magazine was a gigantic success. The book line was a gigantic failure. Good science fiction authors could at last appear in hardcovers by 1950 and Gold's offer of $500 for a novel in a digest paperback format was sneered at. Only a handful of original novels appeared in it. Hindsight gives him credit for buying the Novel That No One Wanted, at least by the more than thirty publishers to whom Arthur C. Clarke sent his first novel, *Prelude to Space*. Nobody bought that paperback at the time either.

Even so, Gold kept the Galaxy Novels alive through multiple deaths through 1961. The first thirty-one were digest size. Numbers 32–35 were a nearly invisible mass-market line called Galaxy. Weirdly, No. 36–46 were issued by mass-market sleaze publisher Beacon, with lurid covers and blurbs that somehow

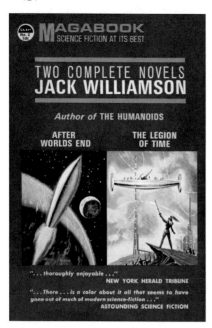

Magabook No. 2, 1963 *After Worlds End/ The Legion of Time* by Jack Williamson. Cover by Ed Emshwiller.

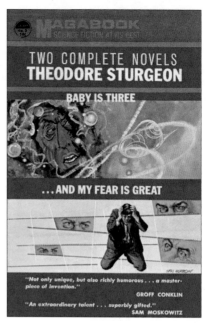

Magabook No. 3, 1965 *Baby Is Three/...And My Fear Is Great* by Theodore Sturgeon. Cover by Gray Morrow.

made Poul Anderson sound sexy. The obsession might have been a schlock horror movie tagline: He Was Compelled to Publish to the Last Dregs of His Blood!

Weirdest of all, the numbering stopped but the alien mind control didn't. When Gold grew too ill to continue, Frederic Pohl took over the magazine and made it good again after Gold's dismal last few years. For reasons impossible to fathom, he too fell prey to digest book madness, starting a new line that absolutely nobody wanted in 1963.

Called Magabook, slugged "Science Fiction at its Best", covers carried a circle containing Galaxy and the book number. The connection with the previous series was made manifest with a three books for $1.00 offer that included titles from the digest line, the mass-market line, and the Beacon brand. Only three Magabooks were issued, each containing "Two Complete Novels" from major names. They were oddly-sized at approximately 7⅛ x 4½ inches; approximately because each is a slightly different length and width, more evidence of how much an afterthought the line was. Presumably a Magabook was a portmanteau for magazine and book, appropriate because the selections had all appeared first in magazines. That anyone thought they could be getting two full novels in as little as 128 pages is doubtful; they were novellas at best. For more on the stories, see Gary Lovisi's "The Galaxy Magabooks," *TDE* No. 4, June 2016. One small correction to Lovisi: the last book came out in 1965, not 1963.

Mercury Mystery

As mentioned above, all modern digests stem from Mercury, the fiction arm of the famous digest-sized magazine, *The American Mercury*. At first it published a variety of types of fiction and even some non-fiction, but the owners soon realized that mysteries sold better than anything else. From No. 35 on, the name of the line changed to Mercury Mysteries. They were the prestige outfit, with a near lock on all the big-name mystery writers: Ellery Queen and Rex Stout, Erle Stanley Gardner and Agatha Christie, Cornell Woolrich and Dashiell Hammett.

Curt Siodmak wasn't a huge name at the time. A German writer who fled after Hitler came to power, Siodmak landed in Hollywood alongside his friend Fritz Lang. By 1942, his name may have been known to insiders as the screenwriter for Universal creature features like *The Invisible Man Returns*, *The Invisible Woman*, and *The Wolf Man* but few in the general public knew or cared. All that changed in 1943, after a 1942 serialization in that famed mystery pulp *Black Mask*, when prestigious mainstream publisher Alfred A. Knopf released *Donovan's Brain*. A doctor salvages the brain of a fleeing criminal and keeps it alive in a glass tank. The brain takes over the doctor's body, forcing him to commit worse and worse crimes. A mystery? No. Even calling it a thriller is a stretch. Horror is a better term, but since the fake science is better than Jameson's the book has been adopted by the F&SF community.

Siodmak had intended the story as an original screenplay, but producers laughed it out the door as too

Mercury Mystery No. 87, 1945 *Donovan's Brain* by Curt Siodmak. Cover by George Salter.

wild for the public. The public disagreed. The book was an immediate success and therefore immediately bought by Hollywood for far more money than Siodmak had previously asked. It appeared as *The Lady and the Monster* in 1944. And as *Donovan's Brain* in 1953. And as *The Brain* in 1962. And as an Orson Welles radio play on *Suspense* in 1944, reprised by John McIntyre in 1948. And in a cheap hardback edition, an armed forces paperback edition, half of a reprint magazine, a mass-market edition, and several foreign language editions. And as a Mercury Mystery. Siodmak went on to write zillions of screenplays for horror/SF films (though, oddly, no adaptations of *Donovan's Brain*). After he grew tired of rehashing monsters, he wrote a sequel to the book called *Hauser's Memory* in 1968 (made into a tv movie in 1970) and a third volume, *Gabriel's Body*, in 1991.

Universal Giant No. 5, 1953 *The Sinful Ones* by Fritz Leiber (b/w *Bulls, Blood and Passion* by David Williams).

Universal Giant/Royal Books Giant

What's with the F&SF titles being issued in weirdly-sized digest formats? Because Universal Giant, launched in 1952, is a thing unto itself. The line issued books that were about 7 x 5 inches, although each title was a hair different in size. And they were fat, up to a full inch in thickness, the first digests to be fatter than *Seven Footprints to Satan*, equal to three of the normal-sized 7⅝ x 5⅜ inch, 128-page Mercury digests. They cost a full 50¢, although other digests had gone up to 35¢ by the 1950s. Buyers got their money's worth. The Giants (usually) boasted that their titles were complete and unexpurgated. Seven of the eleven Universal Giants contained two full novels, the rest encompassing one huge novel of a sort that no other digest would touch because cutting it from 300 pages to 128 pages would have ruined it. For no apparent reason, the name changed

to Royal Books Giant with No. 12, skipped No. 13, and struggled on through No. 29. Seven of those books were issued in a taller format, 7⅞ inches, with widths ranging from 4¾ to 5 inches, again not a size seen anywhere else. Some had type so tiny that they crammed in 200,000 words of fiction, equivalent to four normal digests. Royal Books disappeared in 1954, it and the Universal titles remaindered and sold for 9¢ each at drugstores. At the same time Universal Publishing & Distributing (UPD) discontinued all its other digest-sized lines, like Uni-Books, Intimate, and Stallion, and started the mass-market sleaze line Beacon Books. That prescient move signaled that the era of the digest novels was coming to an end. Mercury was the first and last, not giving up until 1958 when it converted into a digest magazine.

The Giants printed no true science fiction, but several fantasies and fantasies-by-courtesy appeared. Talbot Mundy wrote historic novels of grand adventures, some of which concerned secret societies and other fantastic elements. *Jimgrim*, reprinted here as *Jimgrim Sahib*, the first of the Giants, is closest to fantasy of the five Mundy books Universal reprinted but it's still basically an exotic adventure.

Fritz Leiber's *The Sinful Ones* is an original reprint, an oxymoron that demands explanation. The story had originally been planned for John W. Campbell's *Unknown Worlds* fantasy magazine, but that got dropped when the war cut paper allocations. After the war, Leiber tried expanding the story to 75,000 words but couldn't place that either. Finally, he rewrote his earlier

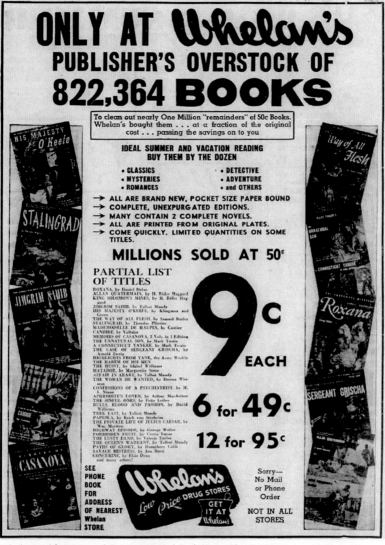

Whelan's ad for Universal Giants, *New York Daily News* July 13, 1954.

steps toward publishing it as a separate genre were in those early days. When doing historical analysis, I always remind myself that looking at what is *not* there is often as revealing as what is. The paucity of SF in digest novels (and the total lack of woman writers of either SF or fantasy) makes a statement. The world would change dramatically just a few years later; too

late for digests which mostly faded away at around the same time. They are a time capsule of a lost era.

New articles by **Steve Carper** appear regularly on <FlyingCarsandFoodPills.com>. Steve's book *Robots In American Popular Culture* and companion website of the same name are essential reading. His digest novel collection has passed 1300.

Gaslight Unrolling of the Stars

Fiction by Robert Snashall
Collage by Marc Myers

"Variety's the very spice of life . . ."
–William Cowper "The Task" (1785)

"Variety's the very spice of Afterlife."
–Papyrus 69, The Star Scroll (2nd Millennium, BCE)

Night arched starry darkness over the Eastern Seaboard. It was the modern Victorian Age of industry, machine and invention. But there was only so much the dingy gaslight illuminated in the shadowlands of the dockyards. Fortunately, plug tobacco had come into its own.

Jossun "Joss" Strobbe, chawing down on the sweet brick plug, couldn't easily roll up his sleeve for the bulking bicep that blocked the way. "Oooo," he admired his muscle, stroking it 'til it pulsed. That hearty got him to where he was today, a constable with stripes—the kind men step aside for and women pine. The regular pay wasn't bad. But he had scrabbled many a year and he was due to get his. He employed the bicep after hours.

Tonight it was loading two long wooden crates at the dock onto a cart for a show at the Boss man's up on the hill. Strobbe noticed the crate stamp: Egypt. "Some more highfalutin junk," he scoffed, "but it pays."

As the cart pulled up, Boss's cart driver coughed, wheezed, slouched over muttering. "Babbling consumptive," Strobbe judged.

Still, Strobbe had to hand it to the Boss. The Man was on top of it. Crates of smuggled loot on a beer cart got past customs and the night crawling Police Commissioner out for a sting.

"Okey dokey . . ." Strobbe, lolling into dreamy satisfaction, spat out the chaw, lit up a smoke.

Pop Pop Ping. That's how it started, nails pelting the street. A crate bucked, rocking from side to side. Boards strained, wretched, splintered. But dammit it was break time! Strobbe woolgathered on. The crate lid rose, flew up, slammed.

Thud! That was just enough to roust Strobbe back to the job.

"Heave," he let loose the bicep doing the work of two men. By the look of them these crates would be weighty. "Gad, one is light but one is not. Nothing for the likes of us." He stroked the bicep bulging. The bicep understood him unlike that hacking half-blind wife, her nose smudged with grime after diving for the odd coin table scraps he tossed onto the oily floor.

"Two crates and done." That deserved another smoke.

His offer of a smoke was met with silence from the driver now standing bolt upright flexing a body reinvigorated. In a dramatic flourish, the driver swished the whip with swagger, a move sure to catch the attention of Strobbe. "Look at him then, all full of himself," Strobbe sized up the driver. "Wonder what's got into him?" Shrugging, Strobbe, hand on the horse's bridle, lit up a stogie. He would release the cart in his own good time.

He settled back into a trance of anticipation. He would be rewarded! There would be boodle for flings with the fillies at Madame Champignon's. He closed his eyes catching the flicker of their lashes over plush red velvet, scented. Perfume, oh how it hit after the heat and stink of the streets. Perfume—ribald, rich, rapturous, oh how it embraced him like no other, save the bicep.

Breathing deep he purged clogged corridors of his cabbaged gut. "Ooooahh!" The scent beckoned him up. Up to the stars. "That's for old Strobbie," he waxed, "one of the stars." The corners of his mouth ascended into a smile, a contortion usually graced with malice.

A shadow silent and slow crept up his body.

"Aab-asbu-aaa-ta-aqa-aatr!"

Moaning. It wasn't coming from him. He wasn't that kind of guy.

Strobbe caught his breath. Actually he caught nothing. There was nothing to catch. A steel pincer throttled his throat. Tightly bandaged fingers depressed Strobbe's protruding voice box. Not a squeal escaped.

Then from the cart it began again. Nail popping, wood splintering, lid rising. The second crate combusted in a flume of an overpowering floral spice, the parting whiff.

Groaning to the gutter, Joss Strobbe and bicep were clawed down from the stars and flung into the abyss, the Primordial Darkness of a goner.

But no doubt about it, the trip was terrific . . .

The driver nimbly remounted. Back on the perch, he was ready to roll, and this time he wasn't alone.

It was morning. Pritchard Middenton awoke in his disheveled lodgings. He itched as if there were no tomorrow. His olive skin left untended scaled down to the bone. He would flake into insanity. It was an inheritance. Mother always had a retinue of glass unguent jars. With long lacquered fingers, she was forever scooping her nails into pools of lotion. She swore by the old tried and true—honey and goose fat—proclaiming, "Lubrication is the staff of life. Stay oiled."

"Right Mumsy." Prichard agreed to himself but the heat was on so he needed a heavy-duty salve to staunch the sweat. The Whalers Treatment, spermaceti and amber-gris, should do the trick. He was ready to visit Mother across town.

He approached her blue painted door dreading tonight's Panorama show featuring bona fide mummies. The crew would set up and operate the Panorama backdrop, a long moving canvas of painted scenery cranked from one vertical roller to the other at each end of the stage. Mother set him up to introduce the show so that he would actually "do something rather than degenerate as an utter wastrel." Mother booked the show full barrel. If it didn't pan out, well, She always kept her powder, unlike her skin, dry.

"Really Pritchie, you look a fright!" Mother greeted with her usual insightful salvo. This was a tad unfair as he was feeling better despite himself and a frightful pallor had shrouded her until just last night. Now she had color full bore. Her dark pupils moved from side to side up and down within the confines of her lidded sockets judging the look of this, her offspring. "I can't see your suspender trouser clamps."

Horrors! The woman had glommed onto his folds of flaking flab drooping over waistline. "How do you manage it Pritchard? You certainly didn't get it from your father's side or mine." Alas, 'twas true, Mother was the picture of slathered svelte, a taut temptress that had slickly seduced father, who was missing in Pritchard's life but slim by all accounts. "Lay off the casseroles."

While Mother perched on her lion clawed throne fronting a blue screen of orbiting beasts, creatures, crustaceans, her talons plunged into a supplicant tureen of lotion. Pritchard announced the business at hand. "My Panorama show–"

"Our Panorama show, Mother's booking dearest," she expertly corrected.

"Tonight at Bilderquart Hall," he mechanically went on, "Tiffington Bilderquart IV hosting in the parlor."

"Yes, I know dear, are you listening? I booked it at Bilderquart Hall. Tiffington Bilderquart, society man-about-town, splendid! Your opening must be strong. The show will be a hit if you don't mumble." She took another scoop.

Pritchard's lament commenced. "According to a note from Perkins, Bilderquart's man, the crates arrived late looking tampered with."

"But arrived they did, contents accounted for!" She brightened. She made it her business to know.

"The show's presenter, Professor D.B. Cheriffe, hasn't arrived."

"He'll show."

"The backdrop cranks are sticking. The crew can't crank the scenery."

"Use that thick whaling grease you're so fond of glopping on to the annoyance of those of us who can smell such as I this instant." Mother gagged.

Pritchard drooped. "Stand tall," she commanded. "Add lotus oil to the crank grease for the sake of the audience. And one more thing."

He could hardly wait.

"Tuck in your shirt."

Taking his leave, Pritchard Middenton stumbled mid-street hailing a hansom cab for Bilderquart Hall. Mired in the tucking of shirttail, distressed folds compacting up his backside, his right arm was stuck helplessly in his crotch. Worse, he had to resort to

hailing with his left—very poor form. Mother would be livid.

Nonetheless, the cab stopped. The driver, poised and adroit, theatrically flicked the whip at the cab's passenger seat signaling to the compromised client where to land.

Up into the cab Pritchard grasshoppered. Seated on the trapped arm, he strove for its dislodgement, his thrusts forcing the cab to lurch this way and that, that way and this. The cab managed to tack to Bilderquart Hall without his having to give directions. Thankfully, the driver knew where to go. The cab's suspension survived.

Upon arrival, Pritchard was tendered at the back of Bilderquart Hall, the performers' entrance, tunneled out of earth and foundational stone, fit for actors, a full story below the servant's entry. Thus deposited, in a desperate burst he freed his right arm sproinging his shoulder.

The parlor was a bustle of activity. On the parlor proscenium stage, the crew was adjusting the backdrop roll. Arriving in time to appear useful, Pritchard dosed the cranks with Whalers Treatment plus lotus. The scenery rolled without a hitch, the first scene adorned with pyramids, palms and pashas bearing the legend: "Egypt Land of Mystery."

Pritchard stood back, transfixed by the sweeping bravura of the scene. As he massaged his aching shoulder, Fushamena O'Rexley, prim household staff stiff extraordinaire, offered him afternoon tea on a platter of pewter, the silver being reserved for guests.

His mind lazing about above the pain in a daydreamy oasis of caressing zephyrs and sweet date wine, his left hand responded in yeoman service lunging for a cup. "Thanks!"

"Arrrgh," O'Rexley reflexed in mortification, pointing underneath platter to the offending paw. The left hand snatch was just not done in polite society not even to the help.

"Dreadfully sorry," Pritchard recouped, managing with beaded brow to lift his right arm that, having in the meanwhile gone to sleep, flopped like a dead fish onto the tea tray upsetting the pageant, sending Fushamena sprawling, screaming, "Wa-hoohoohoohooo!"

The floor was, until then, spotless.

At his painted lady townhouse along the seawall, Finstiddle Parquapshaw Battshtoop relished his situation. It was the evening of the Panorama premier. He appraised the cut of his crisp collared evening jacket, braided Austrian knots looping down silk arms to the oriental arched cuffs. He swooned in a giddy display to his confessor, the looking glass, mirroring the enchantment of deftly applied facial coloring to offset advancing age.

He toasted himself with a Christian cup of steaming creaming Earl Grey tea, his fingers snaking around the handle save his pinky sticking straight out signifying blissful entitlement. He thrived in trade, investing in undeclared cargo at discounted insurance rates. It was He who had the ground game to "procure" tonight's starring relics from the tomb and ship them over duty free.

It was enough just to be him. He was who he was—superior, sparkling in the sun, with a dash of sorcery at his core, the conjurer of the Panorama. "I'll be the popsy wopsy belle of the Bilderquart ball."

Slipping on of doeskin evening gloves completed with a twirl of the burnished raptor knobbed walking stick, Battshtoop pranced out to the awaiting hansom cab. It was of course provided with driver by Tiffington Bilderquart, which was of course only fitting for Battshtoop's station.

He elegantly elevated to the cab oblivious of the driver who was, "after all, only a servant." Did his toes coiffed in calfskin touch the ground? Nesting into the stuffed leather, he and pinky assumed center seat. With the walking stick he flicked a smart tap on the front panel. That signaled the driver, erect and curvaceous, whip crossing over chest, to get cracking.

The deep echoing clop clop of the horses' hooves on cobbles kept a lulling beat in the rain. Battshtoop delighted in looking not out the window but at it. A curtain of soft pelting raindrops rendered the perfect reflection—his face. He was entranced. "So pretty," he fawned.

There was but one thing for it— politics. He would stand for political office. It was only right. He would staunch the stench of low class corruption. He would bring a fresh breeze. Above all, he dabbed dollops of the finest essence behind his ears. He swayed in the smell. "Ahhh!"

The smell. Oh, the smell. It grew, transformed, overwhelmed. The cab stopped, a shadow loomed. None of this broke Battshtoop's attention away from Himself.

"Wenem-bau-sen-eb-ti-er-per-ek!"

He acknowledged his due, "Quite so, spirits moan in admiration!"

He marveled at how potent he was, so much so that he bubbled up starry eyed beyond his usual refinement in a burst of—emotion.

No, it wasn't emotion quite. But he did choke up. Slender fingers dripping bandages crawled up his chest. Curving nailed fingertips ripped open his collar. They smelled divine. A vice cradled his head squeezing. As resinous thumbs plunged into his cheeks, depressing down down through layers of blush, he shot a last adoring glance at the mirroring window. He looked perfect, except for one teensy detail.

His well-outlined lip rouge was splitting.

Confined to cab in a tight spot, the horror of shoddy lip rouge flash flooded all over Finstiddle Parquapshaw Battshtoop. Since it pertained to his look, The Look, his powers of concentration magnified his strength to superhuman levels. He erupted, breaking the throat-tightening grip into pieces, detached bandaged fingers ricocheting all over the cab.

"User-ka-ia-ib-seha!"

Piercing moaning bounced around the cab interior along with the fingers. Battshtoop noticed not. But he had arrived.

Raging with anxiety over peeling lips, he leapt from the cab to Bilderquart Hall. Cowering under collar, he dashed through the entrance on powder room quest spinning Fushamena O'Rexley like a top. Poor dear ruffled Fushamena hardly had recomposed from the left-handed platter affair when she was hit with Hurricane Battshtoop.

But he was a master of powder room touchup. Facial lip reconstruction deftly done on the crapper, Battshtoop resumed the posture of propriety promenading into the parlor to receive Tiffington Bilderquart's salutations.

"Battshtoop, quite right, We are in the pink of health," Bilderquart greeted with the royal stiffnecked assurance of the chosen.

"Yes, well, Tiffington, one must do what one must."

"It will be a deuce of a show— a Panorama of ancient Egypt with the unwrapping of two pristine mummies just off the boat from Egypt to we the living. Bringing the dead back to life, eh? Just your kind of thing."

Battshtoop puffed up at the allusion to his magical presence. "Yes, Tiffington, let's give credit where it's due." Pinky chuffed, Battshtoop paid a compliment. "The staging for a parlor is adequate."

"Yes, we must think of everything Battshtoop."

"Right you are. And so you did. Door to door service, providing the hansom cab and driver."

"Hold on there Old Boy. I did not."

"You did not?"

"Provide cab and driver."

"What?"

"But we do have pineapple juleps. Fushamena, our friend here is a little dry."

Out of the corner of his eye, for lesser breeds deserved no better, Battshtoop saw the servant approach with platter. He reached with his right hand for a pineapple julep. He missed. Not missing a beat, he tried again. He missed again. "I do not miss. This cannot be!"

He deigned to look. He thrust his right out, and just as it was about to grab a glass, Fushamena listed hard starboard to his left. He stuck up pinky to wrap around a glass stem which it just about managed when she keeled portside then rose with an uppercut pouring pineapple julep all over Battshtoop's facial.

"Eiiieeeeya," Battshtoop batshit tore to the crapper into lockdown.

Fushamena O'Rexley tried to aright, but was most badly discombobulated. The medical advice was strapped bed rest and limited exposure to swells.

Battshtoop slunk onto the toilette seat. He was a mess. His visage was so painful to behold he shifted in shock to watch a fly. It buzzed him, looking to lay eggs. The fly's search was short. The insect was consumed in a shadow of shapely human dimensions.

"Agap-ai-khemket!"

A moaning curvy creature wrapped head to toe in linen strips sashayed into the gaslight. Within the depths of where eyes used to be, two obsidian orbs jettisoned lasers mesmerizing Battshtoop who was born to be the center of attention.

Nicely rebandaged fingers seized his head under ears, gold tipped fingernails compressing compressing, lifting him up. He despaired not. After all, his toes weren't touching the ground, and he was treated. The smell was flowery, beguiling, spell binding—an aphrodisiac.

He submitted to this, his and pinky's swan song in the land of the living. "Why fight it when one is out of rouge?"

In ancient Luxor Egypt 1200 BCE, Ptahkaba massaged his head. Another headache was coming on for the Star Priest. The stars were troubled, the universe rumbled. These transmigrations of two

souls 31 centuries into the future were not going well. The Silver Sistrum, the Divine Rattle with golden rods, was shaking on its own power. It was a sign: "We have a mission problem, Luxor." Chaos!

Chaos shook the order of the universe. Chaos upset Hapi, god of the Nile flood. Hapi controlled the flood composed of the tears of the goddess Isis crying over dearly departed consort Osiris. Chaos threatened either high flood washing out villages if Hapi was saddened, or no flood causing famine if Hapi angered. As agent of Pharaoh, may He have life, prosperity, health, Ptahkaba was charged with keeping Hapi happy.

It was up to Ptahkaba, Pharaoh's fixer, to fix it. He would start with the tomb of the transmigrated.

He jumped onto a chariot for a tomb run and mummy checkup. Sure enough, in the tomb of the court impresario Hubbahubba-Instep and his dare to be great wife, Nefernefer-Cuetip, the divine aura of disturbance foretold the desecration of their mummies in the distant future.

"Isis, goddess of magic and wisdom," beseeched the professional wailers hired by Ptahkaba. "Preserve us!"

Mummies looted! Nothing enraged mummies more. They totally lost it. Chaos!

Meanwhile back at Bilderquart Hall, Mildred Winniefredd Peadbunkel, society matron of endowed proportions, played her ace with host Tiffington Bilderquart.

"Tiffington the Season is upon us."

"Mildred, you have my offer?"

"Oh yes, it would be quite the thing—a second unrolling of the mummies for the Ladies Auxiliary of the Knights of the Golden Muleshoe."

They toasted a tertiary round of juleps to seal the deal.

The combined ringing of the servant bells signaled show time. Bilderquart's major domo Perkins gently directed the inebriated to their seats. Winniefredd Peadbunkel extracted her diminutive consort, Cliffbart, Esquire, from auguring exploratory shafts underneath the Oriental rug.

"Oh Cliffie, do be upright," her iron caress sledging him down to floorboards.

"Nyeshh shdear . . ."

Perkins escorting, she set Cliffbart, Esquire, onto a chair. The gas lights dimmed, his feet dangled.

Through parting curtains Pritchard Middenton inched forward to center himself. His heart pounded. It was all he could hear until Ali Baba Scheherazade melodies alluringly drifted out over the parlor via phonograph. The Panorama scenery via lubed up cranks had his back. Words came. But for how long?

"Tonight we will witness the wonders of Egypt. How the ancients defied death, wrapped for eternity. Professor D.B. Cheriffe, eminent authority, is our tour guide through the mysteries."

Pritchard crossed fingers into an arthritic lock. He hadn't seen the Professor during set-up. Worse, the stage lights threw out piercing heat. He looked longingly out at the broad balcony cooled by the starry night. His skin itched something fierce. He ruminated on lotion. That's when he saw Mother take a seat completely obscuring Winniefredd Peadbunkel's little guy. As Cliffbart fell from sight, Mother looked absolutely radiant.

It swept Pritchard back to early visions—memories?—of palmed pools under a sparkling desert dome of stars. It was honeyed, it was calming, it was dark. So dark that he—oh no! Dark! He was in The Black! He went up on his lines. What lines? A little voice inside him asked, "Who am I? What am I doing? What am I supposed to say?" He was one beat from fleeing incognito to a monastery.

Then he appeared, from the wing, stage right—The Professor. He stood sublime, sleek, decked out in white galabeya, gold sash, red fez. The scenery scrolled, noiselessly. In sheer relief, Pritchard boomed— "Professor D.B. Cheriffe!"—an alarm that awoke the nodding off.

The Professor strode out in front of a starry scene of the Egyptian sky. He salaamed the audience. The parlor darkened. From each of the wings, props wheeled in. When the lights went up, two ancient Egyptian anthropoid coffins starred center stage. The audience faced the House of the Dead.

The Professor spoke.

"To attain the Afterlife was the highest wish. The ancient ones had many ways to assure that could be done. It was vital to preserve the body. Mummification was perfected. There was physical treatment, wrapping, ritual feeding. Wherever and however far the soul went, the body must be kept inviolate, the mummy intact. How can this be done with unwrapping, tonight's unrolling? We shall see."

The Professor positioned

between the coffins. He spread his arms wide, palms up. "Rise!"

The coffin lids cracked. The audience leaned forward. The lids were opening as if on their own! "What an illusion!" Tiffington Bilderquart beamed, this would assure his election to the Philosophic Adventurers Society. Creaking creaking, the lids steadily admitted julep-laced air onto the bandaged ancients. The lights dimmed, the audience straining to see, Cliffbart jumping up and down on his chair.

All of a sudden the light from a thousand stars shone bright. Crack! The lids flung open all the way.

"Dear god!" The social register nonpareils at Bilderquart Hall were, though they did not like the word, "collectively," aghast.

Back at Luxor, to pinpoint the problem, Ptahkaba would have to take a closer look. Multiple mastaba levels up, he ascended the stairway to the House of the Stars. There, calibrated grooving sited him through constellations following The Star Path.

The Star Path was the gate taken by the highly honored dead to worlds of their choosing. They could travel to other times and places and become what they wanted. Ptahkaba as Star Priest, the "Star Seeker," had the secret knowledge: That the name of the portal was "The Star Path." That The Star Path was coded within the Zodiac later to be carved on a ceiling of a chapel dedicated to Osiris in the Hathor temple at Dendera Egypt. That as Star Priest only he could rebirth the dead and transfigure select dead into star tripping spirits according to sacred ritual contained in The Star Scroll.

And that was what Hubbahubba-Instep and Nefernefer-Cuetip expected. They lived high. Hubbahubba-Instep staged imported nubile dancing entertainments that left Pharaoh oozing with deelight, "Bully!" Nefernefer-Cuetip managed the business end along with setting up a string of cosmetic stalls in souks down Egypt.

The couple had endowed Ptahkaba's temple in perpetuity. Shazam! They were slated to be Star Spirits, guaranteed! They raved it up overdoing it so, that Nefernefer-Cuetip seed in belly made the journey to the Astral Afterlife many floods ago. Recently, Hubbahubba-Instep followed to continue the hook up. With Ptahkaba at the ritual controls, they were shot into a time and place far, far away.

In the House of the Stars, Ptahkaba plunged into a full migraine. The Star Scroll was unrolled asunder! Rifled spells! He shuddered. Before shuffling off, Hubbahubba-Instep had been poking about the holy of holies. Ptahkaba had to work fast.

He got into the groove, focus detailed by ritual visioning. The coordinates locked on Bilderquart Hall. Ptahkaba blanched. "By Amun, behold hyper manifestations, splayed servant, jumping little guy cult doll, cheesy theater." The portents of disturbance were unmistakable.

There'd be a hot time in the old Hall tonight.

"Look!" Up went the cry. "They're alive!"

The mummies took another step. Professor D.B. Cheriffe invoked.

"Wiu-khepish-tekh!" He smiled wide crocodilian whites. It was shaping up to be a good night. He had the audience in the palms of his hands.

Forward the mummies strode toward the assembled awe-struck who, despite all, noticed attire. "Look! The bandages are brand spanking new, pure white!"

"Ladies and Gentlemen," The Professor introduced the cast, "I give you AmenBicep and AtenPinky."

In his element, The Professor shouted, "Abekh-abu-afau!"

That was their cue. The mummies sprang! AmenBicep, plowed into those right of center aisle, AtenPinky leapt so light of foot at those left.

And that was the cue for the clustered upper crust, which constantly trumpeted class solidarity before the masses, to default. "Every dog for himself!"

The parlor broke up helter-skelter spinning off twisters of sartorial detritus—popped diamonds, frat fobs, silk remnants, hair pieces. As the Professor dazzled, Mother harem danced sinuously around him leaving Pritchard stunned in the dust.

AmenBicep snugly cradled the squealing head of Tiffington Bilderquart in bicep, after shaking hoity-toities upside down by the ankles to carpet the floor with floating stock certificates, which caused further scrambling by crawling tank suckers filching for profit. AmenBicep smooshed tobacco—rolled, pouched, plugged—against his obstructive mouth bandage. This detonated an explosion of frustration. It was the gnashing of his fast loosening teeth—not moaning, he wasn't that kind of mummy.

Meanwhile, spinning the squirming pint-sized squire around on a crystal chandelier arm, AtenPinky indulged a dalliance with Cliffbart. Not that there was no time for reflection. AtenPinky took time-out to primp before all the mirrors, a tricky endeavor given the inconvenience of face wrapping. He made sure pinky was erect, impeccably bandaged.

Yes, The Professor, Mother, and mummies were bringing the house down.

Ptahkaba's temples throbbed. Over the top theatrics brought on by incarnation and reanimation spells lifted from The Star Scroll meant one thing—"Rogue Mummies!" The transported spirits of Hubbahubba-Instep and Nefernefer-Cuetip had merged with their purloined mummies to raise mummies of their own creation.

Ptahkaba had to stop this mummy mayhem, a stellar abuse of power. Kemetmin, Nubian Medjay cop, and his trusty trained baboon both bit it early after terminal scorpion stings but as essential keepers of order they reached the Hereafter's highest heights. Kemetmin and baboon would do the heavy physical lifting to quell the disturbance. Ptahkaba dispatched the Star B-boon Unit.

"Sentamenta-hoho-hotep!" Professor Cheriffe was contented adlibbing. A good director, he gave his actors free rein. While AmenBicep mopped up, AtenPinky took center stage with his whirling dwarfish act. Pritchard, stalk still, played the role of a papyrus plant. Mother, energy flared and belly bared, swooned around the production with flowing serpentine movement. Onto the juleped throng, she wafted a cloud of pure melting blue lotus. Intoxicating!

But all good things must pass. Even in Eternity. A horn whistle blew, Kemetmin and baboon appeared at-the-ready. Tiffington Bilderquart, his skull bicep-bent, looked up at the cop, "Perkins, do tidy up the place, there's a good fellow." Kemetmin frowned, seized Bilderquart's noggin cracking it to the opposite side. "Thanks my good man," a fainting Tiffington Bilderquart whispered redeemed, "for screwing my head on straight."

Mildred Winniefredd Peadbunkel gathered up shreds of her silken train enough to cover her ampleness, poised to make her exit, when Kemetmin's partner bounded over on knuckles and planted a big smacker on her lips. Eyes shut, steam rising after too many parched years when Cliffbart couldn't rise to the occasion, Winniefredd Peadbunkel blissfully bellowed. "Ahhh Finstiddle Parquapshaw Battshtoop, it's been so long!" The moment savored, she opened eyes slowly, to a rakish grey muzzle and swinging simian ass. "Oh Finnie, your facial is off."

It was time for mummy roundup. Kemetmin corralled AmenBicep and AtenPinky, or tried at least. He called in interstellar backup—Ptahkaba's regurgitation of the mouth spells to deprive the mummies of life sustaining food. AmenBicep and AtenPinky collapsed dead at last. Well, not quite. In an unorthodox gambit, shorn of bodily constraints, their spirits glided off linking bicep and pinky, Strobbe and Battshtoop, in partnership, for better or worse, forever. They left behind a pile of linen strips.

"That's a wrap." Professor D.B. Cheriffe closed the production after a run of only one show.

The Professor hugged Mother bathed in the scent of a thousand lotus blossoms. "Show's over my Honeycone." With the arrival of the B-boon Unit of the MPs —the Mummy Police—it was time to sort it.

Hand in hand, the Professor and Mother walked in unified step out onto the balcony. Their eyes fixed on the stars. The firmament parted. Ptahkaba's transmission thundered out basso profundo over the heavens.

"Akhu-afaf-maa-kheru!"

The Professor and Mother became diaphanous each dividing into two parts. The mummy of Hubbahubba-Instep split away at rest leaving the avatar of Hubbahubba-Instep, the Professor, who rematerialized with panache. The mummy of Nefernefer-Cuetip split away at rest leaving the avatar of Nefernefer-Cuetip, Mother, who reappeared decked out to the nines. The Professor and Mother had been able to assume avatar or mummy or comingled forms with a little help from the Star Scroll. Along the way, they picked up new skills like driving a beer cart and cab.

"Mom? Dad?" Pritchard was gobsmacked. He watched the transfigurations. Here were his parents together or at least their parts, a reunion for which he never dared to hope. But mummies? He was the child of mummies? He itched and flaked.

The Professor soothed without lotion. "Don't fret son, it is we three as embodied Spirits that will live on together."

The coffins once again harbored their rightful occupants, the secured mummies of Hubbahubba-Instep and Nefernefer-Cuetip with seed. Kemetmin would book them back to Egypt, mummies repatriated to their homeland.

Pritchard quickly found the true voice of a son. "Hey Dad can you arrange a grand tour of ancient Egypt for me? Just one day there I would be the greatest Egyptologist ever," he gushed brushing aside his Pop's chops, "awarded a university chair, fully endowed!"

"We shall see son. Luxor has to be brought into the cartouche loop."

"Make sure and comb your hair," Mother took over. "Watch the dandruff."

And of Ptahkaba did they worry? No denying, they tipped their spiritual hand in the Panorama to the madding crowd. Yet the survivors soused on lotus laced juleps would remember nothing, and even if they did have glimmers it was not done in their set to say so. That the hearts of the gallivanting Star Spirits testified to their purity in protecting their mummified bodies was a big plus. No, though the Bilderquart frolic was a rough tumble, Ptahkaba would give this Star Family some Star Slack.

Besides, they were already good and dead, the order of the universe restored, the waters of the Nile rising just so—and that was something to be happy about.

Robert Snashall is a DC outsider used to straddling the fault line. When not wrapped in Rose City weeklies, you'll most likely find him at Vista and Spring inhaling a Caesar.

"They cut our budget. This is the best we can do."

Robots in American Popular Culture

STEVE CARPER

7" x 10" 300 pages
McFarland Books, June 2019
Trade Paperback and Kindle

Companion Website

Rock and a Hard Place No. 3
Review by Richard Krauss

"Rock and Hard Place Magazine exists through the support of a community of writers, artists, and supporters who believe, as we do, that stories of struggle help us overcome differences and connect as a society."
–RHP Editorial Board

The third issue of this anthology series opens with a heartfelt dedication to one of its founders, John Lewis Elliott, who "died after a lengthy and courageous battle with persistent health issues. He was 38 years old." The dedication is accompanied by a beautiful illustration of Mr. Elliott.

Following the contents, Associate Editor Albert Tucher provides an editorial triple threat introducing the editorial staff, the late John Elliott's continuing influence on them, and a little inspiration for Covid-weary readers, writers, and booksellers.

Chicken by Jeremiah Kniola
The sensitive younger brother of a kick-ass marine, Chuck, struggles between the machismo expectations of his old man and his own inner voices. "I admit seeing blood made me woozy. A prick from a thorn bush would start my head spinning. I've seen Dad and Chuck kill chickens before, but I've never developed a stomach for it; the systematic extermination of our feathered friends attributing to my aversion to meat." The boy attempts to live up to external pressures ends in failure, disappointing the old man and himself. Only his ally, his mother, does her best to help him get through adolescence, but there's no doubt it'll leave marks.

Off the Road by Claude Lalumière
Supporting characters in stories—waiters, cab drivers, desk clerks—often go unnamed. Their roles, often devoid of personality, define them. They serve a minor,

though necessary, purpose in the action. However, in Lalumière's three-pager, the roles of his three main characters are pivotal, and I'm not about to spoil the fun by calling them out. Suffice to say their characters are suitably defined, the roles each one plays driving their journey and final destination. An off-road joyride to Hell.

Far from Noir: A Tribute to Jonathan Elliott
by the *RHP* Editorial Board

As a newcomer to *RHP* and Mr. Elliott's work, I'll step back and excerpt the board's sentiments:

"He believed in people more than they believed in themselves and he boosted them, like some monoped (his words), wise-cracking rocket that helped you reach escape velocity from your own apathy and self-doubt."

Dig Deep the Midnight Furrows
by C.W. Blackwell

Down yonder, backwoods, where the banks still hold their high and mighty deeds over dirt farmers' heads, Dean Brewer figures a sweet payback deal to cash in on the bankers' past excesses, and save his old man's farm. Blackwell puts you smack dab in Sevier County, Tennessee, rooting for his ragged underdog, no matter his methods—cops and feds be damned. If only life could fade out as sweetly as this neoteric noir.

He Will Kill You by Jen Conley

"I'm so sorry I said those terrible things. I'm so sorry I messed up. I'm a terrible person. Please forgive me." Despite the scars rewarding her loyalty, a serial abuser gets another

chance from his girlfriend. What sets her story apart is the sage advice of the battered women who haunt her fevered dreams. They weren't smart enough to take their own advice but maybe this time, she will.

Made in China
by Alexandros Plasatis

Cultures clash when Pavlo's Greek mama, Kyra Lena, visits for Christmas. Kyra Lena's first impression of Pavlo's Chinese girlfriend, Huiyin, appears positive. But the young woman's behavioral/cultural quirks quickly abrade expectations, and things turn ugly. The crime here is prejudice, closely examined and raw. Do we embrace it and attempt change, or dig deeper into the miserable comfort of a familiar past?

The Parking Lot
by Richard Risemberg

The tang of prejudice in back to flavor Risemberg's story of those

Call this issue a hat trick of desperation. *Rock and a Hard Place 3* continues the chronicles of people who might make one good decision if they could catch a single break.

living on the fringe. A couple of couples eking it out in their RVs, tucked into the corner of a supermarket's lot, fear banishment should their little encampment attract others. When the first tent appears overnight, they fear the party's over. No crime, no foul. A poignant reflection on high-end homelessness and those even less well off.

Portsmouth Naval Shipyard photo essay by Rob Tucher

A photographic tour of the decommissioned naval prison known as "the Fortress," built on the banks of the Piscataqua River in Maine. The prison was used for location shots in the film *The Last Detail*. Tucher's tour is eerie and harsh, just like you'd expect of the "Alcatraz of the East."

Repeat Offender by L.R. Casazza

A possible future where offenders are tagged and monitored, put to work in the berry fields for a roof over their heads and a credit system that provides a meager purchasing capacity. A bleak landscape courtesy of corporate excess and the degradation of humanity. In this vision, it's only the haves and the have-nots— the middle class is non-existent.

Mr. Important by Todd Robinson

A freelance delivery man doesn't appreciate his current egomaniacal boss, who tasks him with delivering loan money to various

clients. He tolerates the self-serving dickwad until a client gives him a good reason to take things in a new direction. Excellent writing and character development.

Barn Find by Robb T. White

A boxcar bandit follows his ex-girlfriend, Carla, and her new sugar-daddy to a ramshackle barn where the old man buys a classic GTO: "pillared cope, the XS option of a factory Ram Air set-up, and the high-lift cam" for a mere $9,700. He wanted it before, but this swindle pisses off our bandit-cum-hero so bad he's now adamant to pinch this buggy first chance he can. Unfortunately, he's out of his mind, and his league. Another satisfying foray into felonious judgment.

In Real Life by Alison Garsha

A transcript of text messages between a stalker and his prey provides an inside look at how a purported high school senior ingratiates and manipulates his victim into a meeting in real life. The progression evokes genuine creeps as the exchange devolves. The outcome is reported afterward in a news report and email.

Between a Habit and a Dream by Mark Krajnak

Two pages of verse about plans gone awry, a missed connection, and losses learned.

Lost Dog Dreams
by Gabrielle Nelson

Each character in this trailer park tragedy comes to life in their own unique mix of hope and despair as they navigate life's hard knocks. The lost dogs of the title belong to Ramsey's mom, who ran a kennel and sold puppies before she packed everything up and left years ago—whereabouts unknown. Now she's just one more skeleton haunting Ramsey's dreams.

Fun with *RHP*'s "Violent Vocabulary" provides a one-page puzzle challenge to match terms like "Avunculicide" with their definitions.

Portrait of Temptation
by Donald D. Shore

Shore pays homage to the femme fatales and patsies of classic paperback noir in this hardboiled potboiler. Although the road may look familiar, this fast-paced seduction into dreamland remains fun, fervid, and, inevitably, fatalistic.

In Need of a Heart in Texas
by Tammy Euliano

Convenience and coincidence converge when a young transplant recipient's mother trades morality for expedience to secure the proper donor for her son. Euliano aligns the elements to evoke the emotional response she's after in this handmade conundrum, topped with a twist you may or may not see coming.

Oscar Montoya Leaves
by David Rachels

We don't know what triggered Oscar's loss of reality, but as it slips from his mind, he grants readers an inside view of exactly what's on in his head—all two brains' worth. A fascinating, first-person study of sudden mental failure and the victim's hubristic attempt to deny it. The collision with reality is inevitable and imminent. The only question is: How much damage will it sow?

The issue wraps with bios of its editors, writers, and artists. The artists are its photographers, who provide stark, haunting images that reflect the mood and tone of the stories.

The *Rock and a Hard Place* tag line "A Chronicle of Bad Decisions and Desperate People" aptly sums up the package. The stories here are often crime and often noir, but the magazine also explores characters who may not be criminals in storytime, but I wouldn't be surprised if they took the plunge somewhere down the line. A great collection of trouble and its aftermath, well worth the support of hard luck story lovers.

Rock and a Hard Place Magazine No. 3
Spring/Summer 2020
Editor-in-Chief: Roger Nokes
Managing Editor: Jay Butkowski
Producing Editor: Jonathan Elliott
Associate Editors: Nikki Dolson, Katrina Robinson, Albert Tucher
Production: Christopher Nokes
Visual Artists: Richard Risemberg, Andrew Novak, Jay Butkowski, Stephen J. Golds, Rob Tucher, Mark Krajnak, Diane Krauthamer
Cover: Andrew Novak
6" x 9" 176 pages
Print $12.99 Kindle $2.99
<rockandahardplacemag.com>

Robert A.W. Lowndes and the Blue Ribbon Legacy

Article by Vince Nowell, Sr.

The word "prolific" is rarely applied to an editor. However, in this case, Robert Lowndes has earned that sobriquet by the multitude of magazines for which he was at the helm.

The Lowndes story is preceded by yet another editor's name: Charles D. Hornig (1916–1999). Hornig was Hugo Gernsback's choice to edit *Wonder Stories* in 1933, when Hornig was only seventeen years old. He was thus nicknamed the "Boy Wonder." Gernsback, who had founded the first all-science fiction magazine, *Amazing Stories* in 1926 (I note this as a reminder for non-SF readers, and those who are far younger than I), needed an editor and chose Hornig based on the quality of the young man's fan publication (fanzine), *The Fantasy Fan*.

Hornig could be a bit of a tough guy with whom to work. He argued with fans in the letters column and at one point printed a declaration that *Wonder* would no longer take ads offering science fiction magazine back issues because such paper goods carried germs. He would have fit right in with our pandemic.

By 1939, the now twenty-three-year-old was an editor at Blue Ribbon Publications, one of the many firm names associated with Columbia Publications. Hornig edited—among many other titles and genres—a pulp entitled simply *Science Fiction*. It kicked off in 1939 and was destined to have a long life as magazines go in the SF world.

Science Fiction had two SF companions: *Future Fiction* and *Science Fiction Quarterly*. That was the status by April 1941 when a new editor showed up. His name was Robert Augustine Ward Lowndes (1916–1998). Going at first by the name "Robert W. Lowndes," he added his initial and was known as Robert A.W. Lowndes after WWII. But actually, he was mostly called "Doc" Lowndes.

Lowndes was not a sure-enough "doctor," like John D. Campbell, Jr., editor of *Astounding Science Fiction* (later titled *Analog*), who held a real Ph.D. Unable to find the reason for the sobriquet "Doc," I asked my friend Mike Robertson, who lives in Maple Valley, Washington. He replied:

> . . . *Robert Lowndes earned the "Doc" nickname from his friends after they learned he'd worked as a porter in a hospital*

Science Fiction Quarterly Feb. 1952 (pulp). Cover story, "Intervention," by Lowndes (written under his Michael Sherman byline), art by Milton Luros.

in the late 1930s. Lowndes had a bucketful of pseudonyms. They included: Doc Lowndes, Sir Doc Lowndes, Jacques DeForest Erman, S.D. Gottesman, Carole Grey, Carl Groener, Henry Josephs, Mallory Kent,

Paul Dennis Lavond, Wlfred Owen Morley, Richard Morrison, Michael Sherman, Peter Michael Sherman, and Lawrence Woods. Almost rivals Ray Palmer, doesn't it?

I see Lowndes standing out

from the crowd in several areas.

1. Longevity. "Doc" Lowndes worked as an editor—and fill-in writer—for over thirty years nonstop, and his magazines survived.

2. He wrote some of the most interesting editorials I've had the pleasure of reading in science fiction/fantasy magazines.

3. He edited at least eight SF/Fantasy magazines, of which all but one were digest-sized sooner or later.

Here's a look at Lowndes' editorial start and a helpful guide (I hope) to issue identification and sequences for the collectors out there:

Columbia Publications starts with SF Editor, former Gernsback "Boy Wonder," Charles D. Hornig

March 1939	*Science Fiction* Vol. 1 No. 1
November 1939	*Future Fiction* Vol. 1 No. 1
July (Summer) 1940	*Science Fiction Quarterly* No. 1

Robert W. Lowndes becomes Editor at Columbia Publications in April 1941

September 1941	Columbia merges *Science Fiction* (12 issues to June 1941) Vol. 2 No. 6 and *Future Fiction* (6 issues to August 1941) Vol. 1 No. 6
Thus:	*Future* combined with *Science Fiction* (6 issues) Vol. 2 No. 1–6
October 1942	Retitled: *Future Fantasy and Science Fiction* (3 issues) Vol. 3 No. 1–3
April 1943	*Science Fiction* (*Future*) (2 issues) Vol. 3 No. 4 & 5
April 1943	*Science Fiction Quarterly* mothballed after issue No. 10*
July 1943	*Science Fiction* (*Future*) mothballed after Vol. 3 No. 5 (17 issues)

End of first sequence until after World War II

May 1950	Columbia Starts Two New Magazines
May 1950	*Future* combined with *Science Fiction Stories* Vol. 1 No. 1 to Vol. 2 No. 4
May 1951	*Science Fiction Quarterly* (starts over) Vol. 1 No. 1
January 1952	Retitled: *Future Science Fiction Stories* Vol. 2 No. 5–6
May 1952	Retitled: *Future Science Fiction* Vol. 3 No. 1 & 2
September 1952	Retitled: *Future Science Fiction Stories* Vol. 3 No. 3
November 1952	Retitled: *Future Science Fiction* Vol. 3 No. 4
December 1952	Columbia launches new magazine: *Dynamic Science Fiction* (6 issues) Vol. 1 No. 1–6
December 1953	Columbia begins new series (digest size—an early convert): *Science Fiction Stories* Winter 1953 (unnumbered)
June 1954	*Future Science Fiction* also converts to digest size
(?) 1954	*Science Fiction Stories* No. 2 and *Future Science Fiction* (October) Vo. 5 No. 3 (final issue)
January 1955	*Science Fiction Stories* continues *Future* numbering Vol. 5 No. 4 to Vol. 6 No. 1 *Future Science Fiction* goes to whole numbers No. 28–48
September 1955	Columbia Publications retitled *The Original Science Fiction Stories* (3 issues that resemble fanzines) Vol. 11 No. 2A–4
February 1958	Columbia terminates *Science Fiction Quarterly* after 28 issues Vol. 5 No. 4 (final issue)
April 1960	Columbia terminates *Future Science Fiction* after 48 issues No. 48 (final issue)
May 1960	Columbia terminates *The Original Science Fiction Stories* after 38 issues Vol. 11 No. 4 (final issue)

*Note: *Science Fiction Quarterly* was the last true SF pulp magazine.

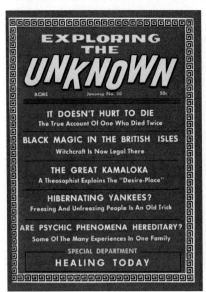

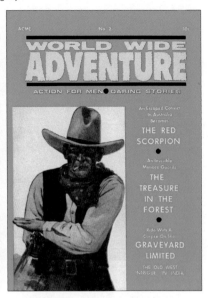

Exploring the Unknown No. 50 Jan. 1969.

Wolrd Wide Adventure No. 2 Spring 1968.

Wollheim's *Stirring Science Stories* for February 1941, and reprinted in Lowndes' *The Magazine of Horror* Winter 1965/66) and "The Leapers" (which he ran in his edited *Future Fantasy & Science Fiction* magazine in December 1942). In 1953, he collaborated with James Blish to write *The Duplicated Man* which was published as a novel (Avalon, 1959). But he was still best known as an editor of science fiction/fantasy magazines, as well as many other publications, such as crime-fiction, western, sports-fiction, and similar pulp and digest-sized magazines for Columbia Publications.

For some additional history, I am again indebted to Mike Robertson. He emailed me to answer some questions, and to say:

Health Knowledge was publishing in the 1950s. As I recall, they did a Mad-*type magazine in 1958 titled* Nuts. *[I remember that magazine; indeed it was a would-be* Mad Magazine.

-vn] Lowndes' big years for Health Knowledge were approx. 1967–69, as far as published titles are concerned, tapering off until [the] company folded in 1971. A bit of speculation on my part, but I think Lowndes got into the sex magazine/sex publication field, as that area sells well, even in down markets.

Other Health Knowledge 'zines (just to round out the topic) included *Exploring the Unknown* and *Shriek*, as well as *World Wide* [sic] *Adventure*, and *Thrilling Western Magazine*, the latter two in 1967–1969, and which included scads of *Argosy* reprints. The ultimate demise of this publisher, according to Marshall and Waedt (who compiled an index) was the same old sad story of problems with the distributor. They also noted the partial contents of the next-scheduled-issues of each of the five mag titles, two of which even got to the printer, only to die an inkless death.

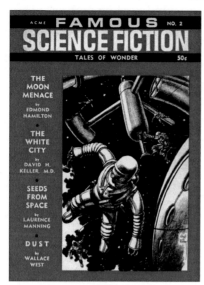

Famous Science Fiction No. 2 Spring 1967. Cover by Virgil Finlay.

Play It Again, Doc!—Robert A.W. Lowndes' Health-y Reprints

In 1963, Lowndes initiated the *Magazine of Horror* (1963–1971) for Health Knowledge Inc., which mixed reprints with new stories. The magazine was popular and spawned several companion magazines: *Startling Mystery Stories* (notable for carrying the first published story by Stephen King), *Famous Science Fiction* (both launched in 1966) *Weird Terror Tales* (1969) and *Bizarre Fantasy Fiction* (1970). Lowndes also brought the works of Edward D. Hoch to the attention of SF&F readers. However, the collapse of Health Knowledge in 1971 ended these magazines. Lowndes subsequently went to work on Gernsback Publications' non-fiction magazine, *Sexology*.

Lowndes received the First Fandom Hall of Fame award in 1991. Recognized as a SF&F historian, he also produced the *Three Faces of*

Science Fiction: SF as Instruction, Propaganda, and Delight (NESFA Press, 1973) 96p, and wrote the "Introduction" for *Dracula* (Airmont Publishing Company, 1965).

In turn, there are at least two major books that focus on Doc Lowndes' life and contributions to the literature. *Orchids for Doc: The Literary Adventures and Autobiography of Robert A.W. "Doc" Lowndes* (with Jeffrey M. Elliot), Borgo Press, Borgo Bioviews No 7, and *The Gernsback Days: A Study of the Evolution of Modern Science Fiction from 1911 to 1936* (with Mike Ashley) (Wildside Press, 2004).

The sixty-eight Lowndes' Health Knowledge magazine issues (five titles) are as follows:

The Magazine of Horror
August 1963–April 1971   36 issues
Startling Mystery Stories
Summer 1966–March 1971 18 issues
Famous Science Fiction
Winter 1966–Spring 1969   9 issues
Weird Terror Tales
Winter 1969–Fall 1970   3 issues
Bizarre Fantasy Tales
Fall 1970–March 1974   2 issues

Why so many titles? My assumption is there was so much material available to be reprinted that it took several different magazines to use up the "incoming" pile. But when I look at the material reprinted, I can see the influence from Lowndes' longtime friend and Avon Publications founder Donald A. Wollheim (1914–1990), whose *Avon Fantasy Reader* set an example for good reprints in digest format in 1947.

As to cover art, I assume it is cheaper to run black-and-white interior illustrations on the covers as opposed to paying an artist to produce a color painting. Lowndes

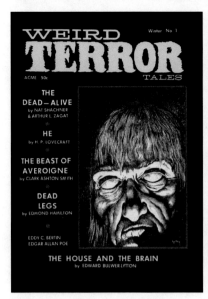

Weird Terror Tales No. 1 Winter 1969/70. Cover by Virgil Finlay.

Bizarre Fantasy Tales No. 1 Fall 1970. Cover by Virgil Finlay.

used this approach to covers in his latter days at Columbia Publications, and certainly on the covers of his Health Knowledge magazines. But when I look at these, I am reminded of some of the many fanzines I read back in the early 1950s. But then, it is the writing quality that counts in the end.

If anyone wants a listing of all 68 issues from Health Knowledge (i.e., story title, author, and original published source, issue-by-issue), my compilation (.doc file) is available at <larquepress.com>.

Acknowledgment

Special thanks to Carole Nowell, my wonderful former school-teacher wife, who proofreads for me. She was especially helpful this article as I am transitioning through double cataract surgery and have a conflict between what the right eye sees and the left eye thinks it sees.

Vince Nowell (Sr.), a sixth-generation native Californian, is a retired technical writer. He has been reading and collecting science fiction & fantasy since 1950.

Before we began publishing *The Digest Enthusiast* in full color (as of No. 11), we tested out the concept with a special edition of the previous issue, labeled Book 10C. This special full color version is available for collectors exclusively from <Lulu.com>.

Stark House Press

PETER ENFANTINO
& JEFF VORZIMMER

The Manhunt Companion
978-1-951473 $19.95

The complete issue-to-issue guide to
Manhunt Magazine—January 1953
to April/May 1967—with story and
author indexes. March 2021.

JEFF VORZIMMER, EDITOR

The Best of Manhunt
978-1-944520-68-7 $21.95

The Best of Manhunt 2
978-1-944520-68-7 $21.95

STARK HOUSE PRESS

1315 H Street, Eureka, CA 95501
707-498-3135 www.StarkHousePress.com

Available from your local bookstore, or direct from the publisher.

THE BEST IN MYSTERY
AND NOIR FICTION

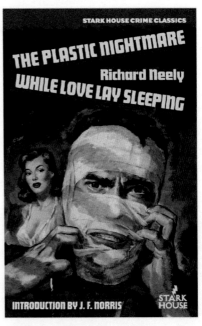

DAY KEENE
Dead Man's Tide/
The Dangling Carrot/
The Big Kiss-Off
978-1-951473-19-8 $21.95

"Tight, no nonsense prose. Terse, vivid dialogue. A plot that grips you on page one and keeps squeezing all the way to the finish."
—Evan Lewis, *Forgotten Books*.
New introduction by Cullen Gallagher.
January 2021.

RICHARD NEELY
The Plastic Nightmare/
While Love Lay Sleeping
978-1-951473-21-1 $19.95

"As noir as noir can be..."
—Ed Gorman. "Richard Neely specializes in the novel in which nothing is what it seems."—Bill Crider. New introduction by J. F. Norris. February 2021.

"...the California publisher that has made a specialty out of returning old and forgotten crime novels to print."—Michael Scott Cain, *Rambles*

Opening Lines

Selections from the digests featured in this edition.

"The village of Shannon wasn't big enough for two funeral parlors, Sam Potter thought morosely."
"The Competitors" by Richard Deming
Manhunt February 1955

"Mommy partied hard and promised that being homeless was only temporary."
"Aileen of Savanne Road" by Nathan Pettigrew
Switchblade No. 12 July 2020

"Muffled drums beat out a nerve-scratching rhythm and red lights flickered hypnotically in the underground Temple of Hates, where five thousand ragged worshippers knelt and abased themselves and ecstatically pressed foreheads against the cold and gritty cobbles as the trance took hold and the human venom rose in them."
"The Cloud of Hate" by Fritz Leiber *Sword & Sorcery Annual* Winter 1974/75

"She was cleaning fish by the kitchen sink when I climbed through the window, my .45 in my hand"
"Kiss Me, Dudley" by Hunt Collins
Manhunt January 1955

"Zeller put the ax behind the furnace out of sight, the long handle leaning against the side of the furnace."
"The Axe" by Ben Hecht *The Saint's Choice* Volume Two 1945

"Back when I was a badge, I didn't have much sympathy for the people I arrested."
"Escape from Sanctuary" by Allen M. Steele
Asimov's Nov/Dec 2019

"When he was thunder in the hills the villagers lay dreaming harvest behind shutters."
"Horseman" by Roger Zelazny *Sword & Sorcery Annual* Winter 1974/75

"My name is Lalo Dias. Long ago, before I became a killer for hire, I was given the nickname Cuban Pete, after the Desi Arnaz song."
"They call me Cuban Pete" by Andrew Miller
Switchblade No. 12 July 2020

"They were sitting in the living room, protected from the menacing darkness by the warm and friendly glow of the TV set—two people who, after six years of marriage, had grown more used to seeing each other in this than any other light."
"The Night the TV Went Out" by George H Smith *Future Science Fiction* April 1958

"The town knew Bailey in spite of the mustache, the lost weight, and the yellowish tan he'd acquired after three years building roads for PanAm Oil in the torrid lowlands of Venezuela."
"Welcome Home" by G.T. Fleming-Roberts
Manhunt March 1955

"Ray Ambrose was too dignified to use actual spit when making spitballs."
"It Was a Tradition When You Turned 16" by Eric Cline *Analog* May/Jun 2020

"I have just buried my boy, my poor handsome boy, of whom I was so proud, and my heart is broken"
Allan Quatermain by H. Rider Haggard
Royal Giant No. 18 1953

"When Alphabet Hicks got home a little before midnight, that Thursday evening in October, he found a man waiting for him at the top of the second flight of stairs in the dingy old brick building on East 29th Street."
"His Own Hand" by Rex Stout
Manhunt April 1955

"The motel room smelled like cooked dope and sex".
"From Dusk to Blonde" by C.W. Blackwell
Switchblade No. 12 July 2020

"A tidal wave of grey flannel dressing gown streamed out behind Miss Chard as she bolted like a bewildered mouse across the vestibule platforms from Car Ten into Car Nine."
"Cold Steel" by Alice Tilton *The Craig Rice Mystery Digest* No. 1 1945

"I'm a railroad cargo pilferage specialist by trade."
"Barn Find" by David Rachel *Rock and a Hard Place* No. 3 Spring/Summer 2020

"The old quarry was almost was an almost circular hole, a pit fully one hundred feet deep and with hewn walls that rose perpendicularly from the floor of the man-made crater."
Atomic Bomb by Malcolm Jameson
Bond-Charteris, 1945

"I am sixty-one years of age, and these are the last pages I will ever write."
"The Impostors" by Jonathan Craig
Manhunt April 1955

"On the ship, we sang and danced and drank champagne—yes, even the children."
"On the Ship" by Leah Cypess
Asimov's May/Jun 2017

"Henry Everett, locking his drugstore for the night, noticed the reflection of two men in the dark and glass front of his show-window, and knew at once they spelled Death."
"A Nickel's Worth of Life" by James H.S. Moynahan *World Wide Adventure* No. 2 Spring 1968

"Night had crawled over the city, as a slug over a small fish."
"A Taste of Rain and Darkness" by Eddie C. Berlin *Bizarre Fantasy Tales* No. 1 Fall 1970

Made in the USA
Monee, IL
28 March 2024

55952934R00098